Not Wanted
in Hollywood

Leonie Gant

ISBN-13: 978-0-9942990-7-9

Dedication

To the people in my life who make me smile every day.

Chapter One

I felt the bed dip as I was in that pleasant dreamlike state and felt lips brush against my forehead. I smiled and heard an answering groan.

"I've got to go, Trudie."

I opened my eyes and looked into my idea of heaven. Detective Jake Griffin and I had been together for four blissful months, seeing each other whenever our busy careers allowed us.

"I'll see you tonight," he said hopefully.

I shook my head regretfully. "I've got a late one tonight. Alistair is still shooting and he wants me there."

Griffin looked annoyed. He didn't like my latest client. I work for an agency which specializes in placing staff with difficult employers. You know, the kind of employers who rant at their staff because their latte is not quite the right temperature. These people do not keep staff for very long because most people have a level at which they won't handle that kind of abuse. My specialty is keeping my clients from self-destructing in front of the world.

My latest client was Alistair Hopkins, a pretentious documentary filmmaker who was considered impossible to work with. A former employee had actually created a website which documented the number of staff he went through and the reasons they had quit. Reasons for quitting had included the cameraman who had got himself lost in the African desert for three days. When he was finally found after an exhaustive search, barely clinging to life, Alistair screamed at him for not taking any footage of his fight for survival. Then there was the personal assistant who had fainted during one shoot from exhaustion after working for forty hours straight with very little food. She had taken out a restraining order against him. I had been called in by his manager as a temporary measure when disgruntled former employees started targeting him both online and in real life. So far, I'd worked for him for a month and managed not to get damaged in any way. Alistair said that I was the most efficient employee he had ever had. Of course, the fact he hadn't almost killed me helped me to stay on his good side.

"Be careful and don't let him talk you into doing anything too crazy."

"I won't," I smiled as I came up on my knees on the side of the bed. I, of course, was neglecting to tell him that Alistair's latest documentary had been taking me into the seedy side of strip clubs for the last two weeks, which is where I would be spending this evening instead of with him.

He leaned down and kissed me gently. I put my hands on his upper arms and pulled him towards me as I took the kiss deeper. Griffin pulled away with a groan.

"Do you know how unfair it is that you do that to me just before I go to work?"

"Just want you to remember what's waiting for you," I grinned.

"Believe me, I know and I think about it far too much at work already. Call me if you get home early and I'll come around."

"I will," I settled back in the bed. "Take care, I'll see you later."

A look of hurt flashed through Griffin's green eyes but was covered up so fast I couldn't swear I'd seen it.

"Bye," he clipped out and headed for the door.

I let out the breath I'd been holding when I heard the front door close.

There was the one dark spot in our relationship. A couple of months ago in a moment of high emotion, I had told Griffin that I loved him. What can I say? I did love him. He was everything that I had ever wanted and I had fallen hard. I'm not one to hide my feelings and in my defense he had just made me very happy, twice. Unfortunately he didn't exactly reply in a way that showed he reciprocated those feelings. I understood. Despite my thinking he was pretty much perfect, emotionally the man was a little stunted. His mother had abandoned him and his dad when Griffin was just a baby. His father, Lee, had brought him up. Their relationship was interesting. When I was alone with him, Griffin could talk about anything. I would spend time with his father, Lee, and you could not shut the guy up. I put both of them in the same room and you could hear the crickets chirping. They weren't exactly an emotionally available family. Understanding that and realizing the cat was out of the bag, I continued for a while in the same vein. I didn't say it all the time, but I didn't choke it back either, especially when he was going to work. He was in the LAPD, and that was a dangerous job. My parents had brought me up to live life well and always tell the people you love that you love them, because you never know what the future could bring. After about a month of this though, I realized that I was throwing it out there and he hadn't once sent it back. My pride started taking a battering and I started wondering if maybe I was in this alone. I stopped saying it, not because I wanted to hurt him, just because I got tired of showing my heart and having it ignored. Whenever I felt it now I choked it off and that had created a little distance in the relationship. I didn't know how to deal with it. I'd kind of made a mess of things and I didn't know how to fix it. Every now and again I'd see a little hurt expression flash over Griffin's face and I felt terrible, but I was stuck. Despite wanting to be with him I was taking back to back jobs with long hours, trying to avoid the emotional quagmire I seemed to have got myself into the middle of. I sighed as I got ready for the day.

That morning I had promised Griffin's father that I would take him to pick up his car from the mechanic. When I got to his house, the front door was unlocked.

Here was another difference between Griffin and I. He would knock on the door and wait for his father to open it. Lee had told me that if he wanted to keep me out he would lock the door. As far as I was concerned, that was a perfectly acceptable way for family to be around each other, so I just walked right on in. Some days I thought I had a better relationship with Lee than his own son did.

"I hope you're up, old man. I've got to go to work," I yelled out as I walked down the hallway. Seeing Lee in the kitchen I was surprised at the strained look on his face. I was more surprised that he wasn't alone. This was probably one of the reasons why Griffin didn't just walk into his dad's house.

"Sorry," I apologized. "I probably should have knocked."

"That's fine, sweetheart," Lee said gently.

The woman sitting at Lee's kitchen table turned around and looked up at me. My breath caught sharply. I knew those eyes. An hour ago those eyes had woken me up.

"This is Jake's mother," Lee said softly. "Angela, this is Trudie, Jake's girlfriend."

So this was the heartless woman who walked out on her baby boy and left him unable to tell me he loved me. See, I'm not judgmental at all.

"So, you're seeing my son." Angela raked her eyes up to the minimal effort ponytail and down to my flat heeled sensible shoes, taking in the high necked shirt and shapeless pants I was wearing. I could see I hadn't made a favorable first impression. Hey, I was with her. Even I normally didn't dress like this, but tonight I was working with a filmmaker in a strip club. I needed to be looking as little like the ladies on stage as I could. If that meant I looked like an escapee from an Amish farm, then that was the way I was going. Angela, on the other hand, had the kind of perfect beauty that only came from great genetics and expensive upkeep.

"Angela is here because she wants to see Jake," Lee

said shortly.

Oh, that was not going to work out well. Griffin did not deal well with mothers. He never spoke about the fact that he had a mother. My petite mom who lived on the other side of the world, scared him to death and we are talking about a big burly cop. He refused to answer my phone just in case it was my mother calling. He accidentally answered it once and Mom went into her mama bear mode. I think it may have scarred him for life. She isn't all that fond of him because she thinks he puts me in dangerous situations and that he blackmailed me with deportation back to Australia once. That second part was true which made it worse. Unfortunately, I get myself into dangerous situations. I could see Lee was unhappy with the situation as well.

I plastered on one of my plastic smiles that I use for work, when some overindulged celebrity is screaming at me for not reading their mind. "That's nice."

Lee's features tightened and Angela just stared as if there was something wrong with me.

"I'll come back when we can talk," Angela said shortly and got up and left.

When the front door slammed both Lee and I winced.

"Griffin's not going to take this well," I warned Lee. "Why does she want to see him now?"

"I have no idea." Lee shook his head and started clearing the table of mugs. I put a hand on his arm.

"Are you holding up okay?" I asked gently.

Lee slumped in a chair. "She walked out on me thirty years ago, walked out on us. When I saw her at the door I had trouble breathing. I don't understand. I thought I was over it ages ago."

"You loved her once and she betrayed and deserted you."

"Don't hold back," Lee said wryly.

"You have to remember that because if you don't, your memory will start forgetting the bad things she did

5

and you'll only remember the good times."

Lee looked at me with surprise etched on his face. "You are the last person in this world that I would think would be against love."

"I'm not against love," I said. "I'm against having your heart ripped out and stomped on while somebody whistles a merry tune."

"You really have an interesting way of looking at the world." Lee smiled fondly at me.

"You ready to go?" I asked.

"You going to tell me why you look like you're heading for a convent?"

"Not today."

I was fully aware that if I told Lee about the strip club assignment, Griffin would know in less than thirty seconds. If I could help it, that was not going to happen.

Chapter Two

Several hours later I was reminded why I hadn't told Griffin about my working at this particular bar. When I had started working with Alastair at 'Hammy's Gentleman's Club', I had made the mistake of wearing my normal personal assistant attire. Unfortunately, some of the more regular clientele had assumed that I was one of the new girls going for a sexy librarian look, and that I would start stripping at any moment if they waved enough cash in my general direction. Since then, every day my dress had become more and more conservative, until today's fine effort, which I personally thought should make me seem completely sexless to the men that frequented this club. Unfortunately, as usual, it seemed that I had severely underestimated a horny man's capacity to spot a pair of breasts, no matter how well hidden they were. Waiting at the bar, I had been cornered by one of the customers and, as usual, my boss was nowhere to be seen.

This shoot was seen as more of an undercover documentary. The crew consisted of Alistair, myself and a cameraman who seemed to end up in the stripper's dressing room on a regular basis. Most of the cameras were stationary and hidden around the club. Alistair was famous for what he termed his covert style filmmaking. To my way of thinking, this was fine when you were dealing with crooked corporations and corrupt politicians. I was having trouble with the reasoning for using it in a strip club. I would have thought that the people who frequented places like this would have an expectation of privacy. But no, Alastair was always trying to push the envelope with his work. He was seen as a radical filmmaker, willing to tackle subject matter that the rest of the industry found slightly distasteful. The critics called him brilliant. I had my own words to describe the man.

"So, sweetheart, how much for a lap dance?" my charming companion slurred.

Before I could answer a voice came from behind me.

"Way more than you're willing to pay, buddy."

I didn't even need to turn around to know who was talking. On the fifth day that we had been filming here I had noticed Travis Cooper, investigator to the stars, hunched over in the back of the bar. He had been following the husband of one of his clients to get the goods for a very messy upcoming divorce. The look of surprise on Travis's face when he saw me joking with some of the waitresses as if we were old friends, was a sight that I will always cherish.

My companion took one look at Travis towering over the both of us and obviously decided that my well hidden charms were not enough to risk life and limb. He shuffled off, muttering into his beer. I didn't feel sorry for him. I'd seen him in the bar before. When he got drunk, he got generous. I could already see one of the girls had accurately determined his level of inebriation and was heading in his direction.

"You still coming in here?" I asked, turning around. "I thought your case was finished."

"It is, sweetheart," Travis said, raising a glass to his mouth. "Just thought I'd come in here on my time off, take in a show."

"Really?" I raised an eyebrow. "You're telling me that, considering the number of strip clubs that you invariably visit while chasing after cheating men."

"And women," Travis interrupted.

"And women," I agreed. "You're telling me that you enjoy spending time in these places even when you are not working."

"Not exactly," admitted Travis.

"Then why are you here?" I asked.

"I'm waiting for the moment when you finally succumb to the lure of the bright lights and take to the stage," Travis said, looking up to where the current dancer was doing an energetic turn on the pole.

"Keep hoping there, cowboy," I said wryly.

"I always do," Travis said. "So, why are you out here instead of backstage with your boss, doing whatever it is that you do?"

I looked at the man sourly. "I was sent out to chase after one of the girls that he'd manage to insult."

"Strippers deal with drunk jerks all the time. They develop a bit of a thick skin," said Travis. "What the hell did he say that upset one of them?"

"I don't know," I said, irritated with the situation. "The man is gifted at being rude to everyone he meets. The first day I met him, he told me that my eyes were too close together. I mean seriously, did he need to bring that to my attention?"

Travis looked deeply at my eyes. "They don't look too close together," he said, holding my gaze for longer than I felt was absolutely necessary.

"Don't tell me that," I said. "Tell the man who has managed to reduce several of the women working here to tears due to his insensitivity."

"So, where is the woman he upset?" Travis asked.

I shrugged. "Probably looking for a gun. I tried to calm her down but she just seemed to get more hysterical. I have a really bad feeling that Alistair may be sleeping with some of the girls."

"Why do you say that?" asked Travis.

"Just lately, I've been getting a bit of a weird vibe from some of them and he's been having some meetings with the manager that I keep getting locked out of."

"You want to be in on the meetings with the guy who manages this place?" Travis asked.

I saw his point. Hammy Pollard had tweaked every single one of my female defenses the second I met him.

The man had been the owner of Hammy's for decades, but I am sure there is a way to do that without exuding the sleaziness that this man did. I had been introduced to him the day we started and his first action was to rake me head to toe, as if calculating the amount of money I could bring into his business on a nightly basis.

"No, but they've been yelling at each other behind closed doors. Considering the way this deal is worked out, they both need each other. Alistair needs access to the place and permission for his cameras and Hammy, from what I've heard, needs the money," I said.

"What do you mean, by what you've heard?" Travis asked.

"The girls talk and I listen. Hammy has got some major debts to unsavory people. The girls say that he is working them harder, trying to push them further as to what they will actually do."

"You know, Trudie, there is a reason you get into trouble. You need to learn to keep your nose out of other people's business, especially when you are in a place like this. People who work here and come here do not like having someone poking around in their affairs." Travis had a worried look on his face.

"This from the man who spends his life poking around in other people's affairs," I said quietly. "I'm not asking for information, I just listen. Some of these girls just want to talk to someone who is actually paying attention to them."

"I thought the documentary filmmaker was supposed to be doing that, you know, going behind the scenes, finding out the gritty realism," Travis said.

I snorted. "Alistair wants his name in lights. He doesn't really care who he has to trample to get there."

"Speaking of which," Travis said. "I think that's your boss trying to get your attention."

I looked over and sure enough, there was Alistair, glaring at me.

"See you later," I said to Travis, before heading off to

whatever new torture Alistair had waiting for me.

"I don't pay you to flirt with the customers," he hissed as I walked up to him.

Technically speaking, he didn't pay me at all. His manager had hired me, through my boss, Monique Petit, to keep an eye on him and try to smooth the ruffled feathers that he invariably caused.

"You told me that my services were no longer required and that I should comfort your interview subject, who had become distraught due to your line of questioning," I reminded him. Of course I was using much more professional language than he had.

"Well, where is she?" barked Alistair.

"She was extremely upset and wanted to be alone. She asked to be excused from filming for the rest of the day," I said.

To be perfectly honest, she had suggested that he put the camera somewhere that would prove very uncomfortable, if not anatomically improbable. Of course I wasn't going to tell the man who thought that he was the greatest filmmaker alive that. Usually I find in these cases that honesty is a pointless exercise.

"I need you to speak to the dominatrix. She is still refusing to be on camera without her mask," Alistair grumbled.

"I've already tried talking to her," I said. "She is adamant that her face never appear on camera."

"Well I need you to change her mind, that's what I pay you for," he snarled.

Once again I had to stop myself from reminding him that he didn't pay me at all.

Heading towards the back rooms I heard some familiar yelling. Rounding the corner, I found Hammy with one of the girls pinned up against the wall in a threatening manner.

"What do you want?" he snapped at me.

"Alistair asked that I speak to Amber," I said,

indicating the young woman he had cornered.

"She's busy," he snapped.

This was where my negotiating skills needed to come in. I shrugged in what I hoped was a nonchalant manner.

"I have got an overwrought filmmaker out there," I said, hoping I was putting the correct amount of stress into my voice. "I am trying very hard to make sure that he doesn't pull out of this deal. You know how much money we all stand to lose if he decides to walk."

I could see that got through to him, the mention of money usually did. He stepped back.

"We'll be discussing this later," he growled at Amber as she walked past him.

I followed her quietly back to the dressing room.

"Thanks for that," she said as she sat at a mirror and started putting on makeup.

I sat down next to her. "I wasn't lying, Alistair does want me to try to talk you into being in the film without your mask on."

"It's not going to happen," Amber said quietly.

"I know," I said, "but I had to ask. It's my job."

"You've got a jerk for a boss," she said.

"Your boss isn't exactly Prince Charming either," I replied.

"That's the truth," Amber said. "I just need to get enough money together to get out of here. I just want somewhere that I can be safe. I just want a home that can't be taken away."

"What's Hammy pushing you for?" I asked.

"He wants me to do more for the customers, give them a bit more of the fantasy." She turned to me. "I came up with the dominatrix act so that I could at least keep a bit of distance between me and them. I hate that I've ended up here but I can't seem to find my way out. The problem is Hammy tells me that the way to make more money is to do more, show more."

I nodded, trying to understand. The one thing that I'd

realized talking to these women over the last couple of weeks, most of them were exactly like me. Sometimes the smallest things can lead you down a different path. Amber was a smart girl, trying to survive the best way she knew how. She'd ended up working for Hammy, but so far she had managed to do it on her own terms. The dominatrix act she had come up with was pure theater. It appealed to the clients but it also allowed her a measure of control that some of the other girls didn't have.

Later as I watched Amber on stage I could see her talent. She was athletic and she had a presence. She was able to promise much but only seemed to have to deliver a small amount. I had told Alistair that she was never going to take the mask off for him. He had reacted with his usual temper. Finally, he realized that yelling at me wasn't going to work at all. I was then informed that I needed to put my time into sitting in a back booth of the bar transcribing some of his riveting thoughts on the stripping industry and how it could be used as a metaphor for the American economy. To be perfectly honest, I had no idea where he was going with this, but I would never be paying to watch this movie so it really didn't make much of a difference to me.

After spending an hour trying to type on my laptop while there was pounding music going on in the background and cheering drunk men around me, I soon decided that I needed to find a new location. Travis, who had continued to lurk around the bar, sat down in the booth next to me.

"What are you doing?" he asked.

"I am about to try to find somewhere quiet to work. I think I might go out the back." I started packing up my laptop.

"Can I keep you company?" Travis asked.

"Please tell me you are not just wanting to get a look at naked strippers."

"Really," said Travis. "If that's what I wanted I'd just

stay out here. No, I'm getting a bit tired of all this in your face and just needed a break."

"Then go home," I said. I stopped packing and looked at him seriously. "I know what you're doing, Travis. I know you're worried about me working here and I know the only reason you have spent the last week sitting in a stripper bar is because you are making sure I'm okay. The fact you are doing that makes you, despite all previous evidence to the contrary, a really nice guy. But it's not your job to protect me."

Travis looked slightly embarrassed. "This is not a good place for you to be, Trudie," he said quietly. "If Griffin knew where you were he would have a fit, you know that. I'm guessing it's probably the reason why you haven't told him about it."

It was definitely the reason I hadn't told him. Having Travis point it out to me though, had me feeling even guiltier than I already did.

"Fine, if I can't convince you to leave, you may as well come with me."

I had become very familiar with the backstage area of Hammys. Between calming down women who wanted to kill Alistair for his interviewing style, and stopping the cameraman from doing another impromptu shoot in the dressing room, I had pretty much found all the quiet and private areas in the place. My preferred area was one that the cameraman, Hugh, had shown me. It was a little alcove, not far from the dressing room. It was kind of hard to find and I really did not want to know how Hugh had found it, or what exactly he had been doing in it, but for now it fulfilled my requirements.

"Where exactly are you taking me?" asked Travis as the area got quieter and more secluded. "I'm not complaining but I really think that I should point out that I am not that kind of guy."

I choked on the laugh that came out. "Who are you trying to kid? You are exactly like that kind of guy. I would bet a lot of money that you have led many a wayward young lady into a secluded part of a building."

Travis smiled and I turned back to make my way through the dimly lighted area. Finding a light switch, I flicked it, glanced back at the alcove and froze.

"What?" said Travis, instantly on alert.

I pointed down. There, lying on the floor of the alcove, was Hammy Pollard with a whip that I remembered from Amber's dominatrix act wrapped around his neck.

Travis instantly squatted down beside the body and checked Hammy's pulse. He looked up at me and shook his head. I wasn't surprised. I really didn't think that the shade of blue on Hammy's face was a natural hue. Travis fished his phone out of his pocket.

"I'm going to have to call this one in," he said regretfully, which confused me.

Of course we had to call it in. Dead man on the floor, you instantly called the police and they called in Homicide. All of a sudden I could see why Travis was looking at me with some pity. Even if Griffin was not working this case, I knew how the police worked. He would be told that his girlfriend, once again, was at a murder scene, at a strip club where I had been working for two weeks without telling him. I was so screwed.

Chapter Three

That really horrible feeling you get in your stomach when you know that you have messed up badly, continued to grow as the strippers and bar staff realized that there was something that had gone horribly wrong. It amplified as I had to deal with Alistair and Hugh and explain to them that filming a murdered man as a money making exercise, could be construed by some as bad taste. It became even worse when the police and the paramedics turned up. By the time Griffin strode into the building, his eyes searching everywhere, I felt so sick I thought I was going to embarrass myself right there, in front of the stage where the police had gathered everyone. When Griffin's eyes met mine I saw relief. That didn't last long though. His eyes flicked sideways and saw Travis standing next to me and fury momentarily washed over his features. He then settled into the cold cop face that I knew and really didn't like, especially when it was pointed in my general direction.

If I didn't know that he was mad before, I would have realized it when he and Ramos spoke to every single person in the building, before heading towards Travis and me. By this stage fatigue had overtaken fear as my number one concern and I was yawning widely as Griffin and Ramos walked up to us.

"Are we keeping you up?" said Ramos sarcastically. Usually I am quite understanding with the way Detective Liza Ramos feels the need to subtly point out that I am not one of her favorite people to see at a crime scene. I understand our relationship is based on the whole familiarity breeds contempt mentality. Tonight though, I had spent the last few hours in a state of heightened anxiety. I felt sick and I was really tired.

"How long is this going to take?" I asked, possibly a little harsher than I should have considering the circumstances.

I could hear Travis's swiftly indrawn breath behind me. Griffin's features tightened.

"As you and Mr Cooper were the ones to find the body, we will be requiring you to accompany us to the station for a formal interview," Ramos said.

For a full five seconds, and I do blame the fact that I was tired and sick with worry, I contemplated not going. They couldn't make me, especially if I got Monique's husband, Reggie, to come and perform some of his attorney magic.

Ramos realized quickly where my thought processes were going. "I could arrest you if you aren't interested in coming willingly. I have no problem with doing that."

"I'm always willing, Liza, especially when it comes to you, you know that," boomed Travis behind me.

As he stepped around me he knocked my arm with his shoulder. I looked up to see him raise his eyebrows at me. I got the message. I was being an idiot. If I could just get through this interview I could go home, curl up in bed and try to work out the exact moment when I had started making a mess of things. All this time Griffin hadn't said a word to me. He hadn't asked if I was okay after finding a dead body, he had barely looked in my direction. I knew he was mad but he didn't show it at all. He had simply closed off. I hated when he closed off.

At the police station Travis and I were separated and I was left in an interrogation room while Ramos and Griffin were with Travis. Once again I was given plenty of time to contemplate how much of a mess I had made of this situation. I had felt guilty about not telling Griffin about the job at the strip bar for the entire two weeks, but at no point had I been able to work out how to tell him in a way that wouldn't end up with me arguing with him. I had taken the easy way out and it had come back and bitten me in the butt. Not much I could do about it now. I laid my head on the table and I didn't know whether it was finding the body, the stress of the last few hours or the realization that the day that had started with me happily kissing Griffin was ending so badly, but I could feel tears pushing at the corner of my eyes.

The door to the interrogation room opened suddenly and Ramos and Griffin came through. Both of them looked annoyed. I could understand that. Travis Cooper was gifted in his ability to annoy people and, thanks to his past history with Griffin, I had no doubt that he would have been in fine form tonight. Now it was my turn. Considering the looks they were giving me, I was not expecting to have an easy time.

"Trudie," said Ramos. "I wish I could say that it was a surprise to see you here, yet again, but we all know that I would be lying. Griffin is in this room, but thanks to your relationship he can't really be involved."

I sneaked a glance at Griffin. Considering the coldness of the expression on his face, I don't think anyone was going to believe that he was biased in my favor.

"So, did you want to tell me why you were working at Hammy's Gentleman's Club tonight?"

"I am working for Alistair Hopkins on a documentary film about the strip club culture. Alistair had organized to have cameras set up in the club. The crew consisted of myself, Alistair and the cameraman, Hugh."

"How long have you been working in the club?" Ramos asked.

"Two weeks," I said.

I could see Griffin's jaw tighten.

"What exactly was your job at the club?" Ramos asked without missing a beat.

"Same as it always is. Personal assistant. I did whatever the client needed. I fetched, I carried, I typed, I dealt with those people who wanted to kill my boss and I did my best to blunt his ego."

"Alistair Hopkins was a problem?" Ramos ventured.

"My clients are always a problem," I said.

"Did Alistair ever have any arguments with Hamish Pollard?" Ramos asked.

I had to stop for a moment before I realized that Hamish was Hammy.

"They argued, but then they argued with everyone."

"What kept the relationship going?"

"Money," I said, "pure and simple. Alistair wanted this film to go ahead and he was paying Hammy very handsomely for the privilege of taping everything that happened in that place. I had heard that Hammy was in debt up to his eyeballs, so he was willing to do whatever Alistair wanted, but he wasn't happy about it."

"Do you have any ideas about who would want to kill Hammy?" asked Ramos.

I shrugged. "It could have been anyone. Hammy wasn't the most pleasant human being. I know that pretty much all of the girls could barely stand to be in the same room with him."

"The guy died from strangulation. Whoever did this put a whip around his neck and pulled. I somehow don't see a stripper being that strong." Finally, Griffin actually spoke to me.

"You'd be surprised," I said. "The girls need huge amounts of upper body strength. I've been practicing on the pole and I'm having difficulty just doing the basic moves, because I'm not strong enough to lift my body up that high."

"I'm sorry, I'm going to have to stop you there," said Ramos. "I really want to truly appreciate this moment. You've been learning how to use a stripping pole?"

Realizing what I'd revealed, I glanced at Griffin. He truly looked stunned. At least he couldn't say there weren't any surprises in our relationship.

"Yes, well, we sometimes have downtimes during

filming and over the last couple of weeks I've become friendly with some of the girls. They have a couple of poles in the back of the club so that the performers can warm up before they go out on stage. Some of the girls have been teaching me how to use it."

"I have to say," said Ramos, "since we've known each other, I have become used to your little quirks and the way you get yourself into unusual situations. I know that you and the unexpected cross paths many times. I have to say though, that I never thought I would hear you tell me that you had been working on a pole in a stripper club."

I rolled my eyes. "It was out the back. I never went on stage. All my clothes stayed on. People do this kind of thing for fitness all the time."

"Strange," said Ramos. "I didn't really think you were a fitness kind of person."

I narrowed my eyes. Ramos was enjoying this moment way too much, even more than I would expect. I'm not saying that the woman actively disliked me. I think I was just more of an irritant in her life.

"Why exactly were you going to a secluded area at the back of the club with Cooper when you found the body?" Griffin asked.

I could tell that Ramos was annoyed with him hijacking her line of questioning.

"I was trying to transcribe some notes for Alistair out the front and was having trouble concentrating. Travis has been in the bar for the last week or so, working and keeping an eye on me."

"What do you mean 'keeping an eye on you'?" Griffin interrupted.

"Travis came in one night for work and found me there. He was concerned that I was working somewhere that he didn't approve of, so he's been coming in this week to make sure I was okay."

Griffin's features tightened. I'd given up even the thought of putting a good spin on all of this mess. I screwed up. I knew it, Griffin knew it, even Ramos knew it.

"I decided to go out the back to somewhere quieter so I could concentrate. Hugh, the cameraman, had shown me the alcove when we started there and I had used it when I needed some quiet time, because it was secluded from the rest of the chaos. Travis came with me because he was a bit tired of the club and wanted a break."

"Travis was tired of seeing the naked women?" Ramos sounded disbelieving and when you put it like that I could understand why. I had spent the last two weeks surrounded by men who couldn't get enough of seeing naked female flesh.

"When we got to the area, I flicked on a light and saw Hammy there. Travis confirmed that he was dead and called the police."

"Did you see anything out of place, anyone around, anything at all?" asked Ramos.

I shook my head.

"Had you seen anything earlier in the night that looked out of place?" she asked.

"Earlier I had come across Hammy bailing up Amber about wanting her to do more with her act. I had also heard arguments between Hammy and Alistair but then both those men argued with everyone. In the two weeks that I had worked there I had seen or heard Hammy arguing constantly. If you're looking for someone who wanted to kill him, believe me you will have a list of suspects a mile long."

"How about you?" asked Griffin.

"What about me?" I asked.

"Had you argued with him?"

"No," I said, beginning to get annoyed. "One time he watched me while the girls were trying to teach me how to use the pole and he made some joke about me being better as a waitress than on the stage, but I never treated anything he said as being serious. The man looked at all women as income streams. I didn't fall into that category so I was disregarded."

Ramos slammed shut her notebook, drawing both Griffin's and my attention.

"I think we have all we need for now," said Ramos, looking from me to Griffin. She rose quickly and walked out, leaving me with the man who I could tell was still working his way through some anger.

"Can I go?" I asked, breaking the silence.

"I'll take you home," Griffin said, with a note of finality as if daring me to argue.

A smart woman would have kept her mouth shut. I, of course, never professed to being a particularly smart woman when it came to my actions with the man in front of me.

"I know you're busy, I can grab a cab and find my own way home," I said gently. In my defense I was trying to help. A murder means that Griffin has work. He's a dedicated cop. I know this and I've learned that sometimes I just need to take a step back when he has work to do. Usually he appreciates my understanding. Tonight didn't seem to be one of those times.

He looked angrier at my offer. "I will be taking you home."

He shoved back his chair and stalked out of the interrogation room. I followed behind him. I was not looking forward to this. I almost groaned when I saw Travis was still waiting for me. He looked around Griffin.

"Do you need a ride home, Trudie?" he asked.

"No she does not need a ride home," said Griffin through gritted teeth. "I am taking her home."

For once Travis took in all available cues and didn't push the situation. He nodded quickly. "I'll talk to you later, Trudie," he murmured before walking away.

The ride in Griffin's car back to my home was silent and excruciatingly painful. I knew Griffin was angry and I also knew that it was my fault. I should have been honest with him from the start, so I couldn't really argue the point now. Griffin followed me to my apartment and when we were inside I turned around, ready for the argument that was coming. For a moment Griffin was silent, just looking at me as if trying to work out what he wanted to say first.

He cleared his throat. "So what you're telling me is that for the last two weeks, you have been working in a strip bar with Cooper."

I looked at him keenly, knowing that nothing I said was going to help the situation.

"I haven't been working in a strip bar with Travis. I've been working at a strip bar. Travis has just been turning up for the last week."

Griffin continued on as if I hadn't spoken. "You chose not to tell me this."

"I knew how you'd react," I said.

"How was that?" said Griffin.

"You would have tried to tell me that I couldn't do it."

Griffin quirked an eyebrow.

"You know you would have," I said.

"Would it have worked?" asked Griffin calmly.

"No, and we would have argued. I didn't want to argue. I didn't want to mess things up between us."

"And this is so much better," said Griffin. "The way this all worked out."

"How was I supposed to know that I'd end up finding a dead body?" I said.

Griffin threw up his hands. "Because it's you, you always end up finding the body."

I wish I could argue with him, but as I had been reliably informed by one of the security guards at the agency I worked for, I was beginning to get a bit of a reputation when it came to my ability to find dead bodies.

"I am sorry," I said, because believe me, I was. "I understand that I've messed up and I wish I hadn't. I didn't mean to upset you. I was just trying to get this job done as quickly and easily as I could."

"But of course Cooper knew about it," Griffin said.

"The only reason Travis knew about this job was because he was following a case that just happened to end up at the bar."

"That's what you both say," Griffin said accusingly.

I froze. "What do you mean by that?"

"Stop being so naïve, Trudie. We all know that Travis wants you. I wouldn't be surprised if he turned up purely because you were there."

"It doesn't matter what he wants," I said. "It's what I want that matters."

"Well what is it that you want, Trudie? Really, just tell me so I know."

I took in a deep breath. "Right now, I want you to stop and calm down, because we're getting close to saying something that we can't take back and I don't want that to happen."

"You know what I think," said Griffin.

"I really don't want to know," I said.

"I think that you're keeping Travis around in case you and I don't work out. He's obviously interested in you, you keep him on the line. The second you and I fall apart you go running into his arms."

I stopped the nervous pacing that I had started when Griffin began this line of thinking and looked at him. "What you just said," I said quietly, "was very, very ugly. I would hope that you would know that I would never, ever do something so horrible, not only to you, but to Travis. I thought you knew me better than that."

"I thought I did too," said Griffin.

"Get out," I said.

"What?" said Griffin.

"I don't want you in my home at the moment," I said. "I know I did the wrong thing but I don't deserve what you just said. It was ugly and it was mean, and frankly, I deserve better, so I want you to leave my home."

Griffin looked like he wanted to argue but something

in my face must have convinced him that he'd actually crossed over the line.

"Fine," he said and stalked towards the front door.

I heard it slam. I walked over to it very calmly, flicked the lock, put my back against the door and my knees crumpled. I fell to the ground and the tears started. I don't know how long I sat on the ground crying. All I knew was that I had to pull it together. Griffin and I had argued before but I'd always been pretty sure that we could get past it. At the moment I wasn't so confident that we were going to get past this. I had a shower, cleaned up my tear ravaged face as best I could, sent a text to Monique explaining the situation and fell into bed. Despite my emotional turmoil, or perhaps because of it, I fell into a deep, dreamless sleep. Tomorrow had to be a better day.

Chapter Four

The next morning I was woken by the sound of my phone ringing. I cursed my habit of putting it beside my bed as I blindly slapped the bedside table looking for it without opening my eyes.

"Good morning, ma petite."

"Oh hi, Monique," I said tiredly.

There was silence.

"Monique," I ventured, wondering what I had done this time.

"I just wanted to make sure that you were okay," Monique said.

"Why wouldn't I be?" I asked.

"Well," she said. "I found a text message on my phone this morning. It came through some time last night. Do you remember what you wrote?"

I was still half asleep so I was having a bit of a problem.

"It said 'another dead body, not my fault, men suck.' Do you remember sending it now?" she asked.

"Would you believe my autocorrect went a little wild?" I said weakly.

"So exactly which part is wrong?" asked Monique.

"Technically speaking, the whole thing sounds pretty much accurate. I possibly should have phrased it a bit better," I said.

"What happened?" asked Monique and I had to give her credit for the fact that she was still completely calm.

"I found the owner of the bar strangled to death with the whip from the dominatrix act." Thinking on it, I could honestly say that I had found a line that I never in a million years had expected to say.

Monique sighed patiently. It also said a lot about her that she accepted that explanation completely calmly.

"That takes care of the first two parts. What about the third?"

"Griffin was called in and I hadn't told him that I was working there. He didn't react well," I said quietly.

"A man like that wouldn't," Monique said. "I would expect he was disappointed that you didn't feel that you could tell him everything."

Great. Like I didn't feel bad enough already.

"Although the fact you felt that you couldn't tell him may mean there are problems between you that are deeper than just this one incident," Monique said soothingly.

Monique wasn't exactly Griffin's biggest fan either. During the time that I had known Griffin, he had managed at some point to alienate pretty much everyone in my life. My friends and family weren't obvious about the fact that they weren't fond of Griffin, but they wouldn't exactly be upset if the two of us broke up.

"So, what are you going to do?" asked Monique softly.

"What I always do," I said. "I'm going to go get my car which is currently sitting outside the strip club and then speak to Alistair about what he wants me to do today. As far as I'm concerned I am still working."

"What about Griffin?"

"I apologized last night. He knows that I'm sorry for what I did and he still said some things which I'm going to have trouble dealing with. I'm not going to beg him to forgive me, especially not after what he said." I was adamant. Regardless of how many tears I had shed over Griffin last night, I hadn't deserved what he dished out and I really wasn't looking at getting a second helping.

"Your decision, ma petite, but if you need me for anything just call," Monique said.

This is the reason I love working with Monique. That and the fact not many bosses would be quite so accepting with the body count I seemed to be racking up, as my friend, Jorge, called my unfortunate ability to find the nearest dead body. Of course, in my defense, I hadn't killed anyone myself. Also, none of the bodies had actually been my clients, so I was still not considered the poisoned chalice that I may have been if circumstances were different, and Monique was slightly less patient than she seemed to be.

I had almost finished getting ready when there was a knock at my front door. My heart jumped into my mouth at the thought that it might be Griffin, looking to work things out after the debacle last night. I composed myself before opening the door and made sure I put a smile on my face.

"Men suck," said Crystal.

Swallowing my disappointment, I waved her in and followed her to the living room.

"They really suck," she repeated.

I hoped she didn't expect me to argue with her, because at this moment she was preaching to the choir. That sounded like there was trouble in paradise though.

"So," I said. "What has Edwin done this time?"

"He's agreeing with my father," said Crystal.

That couldn't be good. A few months ago Crystal and Edwin had run off to have a quickie wedding in Vegas after being friends for ages. Crystal is the daughter of a very rich man and she has a very large trust fund, but no thoughts of a prenup had occurred before the marriage happened and Crystal's father had been having a few issues with that.

"So what is Edwin agreeing with your father about?"

"Dad wants Edwin to sign a postnup," Crystal said.

"A postnup?" I queried.

"Yes, it's like a prenup, but you sign it after the wedding."

"Okay," I drawled. "What is the problem with that? He signs a postnup, your father gets off your back and everyone's happy."

Crystal looked at me sourly. "No, not everyone's happy. I'm not happy. The postnup says that there is a possibility that we might break up. I cannot have an out clause. If I have an out clause I may end up like my mother, the woman who has had nine, or maybe ten husbands. I can't keep up. I cannot have an out clause."

There was the problem. Crystal was terrified that there was a part of her that was just like her mother. I could have told her that she was being an idiot. She is nothing like her mother. She's warm and caring and loyal. Nothing like her mother. For some reason Crystal had got it into her head that when it came to marriage and relationships, her genetics were going to win over the nurturing that her father had done.

"He's just trying to do the right thing by you," I said. "Do you realize how lucky you are that you have found someone who cares so much about you, they are willing to do something like this for you? Even though it probably upsets him that your father is focusing on the possibility of you breaking up. You should be grateful that he loves you so much."

Crystal stopped. "What has Detective Dumbass done?"

See, this is why you shouldn't talk to friends when you are in an emotional state. They are able to pick up on the subtle clues in your language and actions. The fact that she was calling Griffin, Detective Dumbass instead of Detective Hottie which was her usual form of address, meant that she had worked out exactly why I was slightly distressed and having trouble seeing her side of the postnup issue.

"The owner of the strip club died last night," I said.

"And considering that this is you we are talking about, I am going to assume that he didn't have a heart attack while watching one of the acts," Crystal said dryly.

"No, he did not," I said tightly. "He was strangled with the dominatrix's whip."

Crystal giggled and slapped a hand over her mouth.

"I'm sorry, that was totally inappropriate. It was just not what I was expecting you to say."

"No, go ahead," I said airily, waving my hand around. "I've been told several times in the last twelve hours about how nobody is surprised that the man died and that I found the body."

"So Griffin is mad that you were working at a strip club and didn't tell him," Crystal said, cutting straight to the heart of the matter.

"And because Travis has been at the club for the last week keeping an eye on me."

Crystal grimaced. "Okay, I can see what the problem is."

I nodded. "I can too and I apologized last night, but then he said some things which were a bit harsh and I kicked him out."

Crystal eyed me speculatively, but I really didn't want to go into the accusations Griffin had flung in my direction. It still hurt pretty badly that he thought I was capable of being that kind of woman.

"So what are you going to do about it?" she asked.

"Nothing," I said.

"Nothing?" Crystal looked doubtful.

I understood where she was coming from. I am one of those people who usually am incapable of leaving a problem unsolved, but I had no idea how to fix this one.

"I need to get to the club and pick up my car," I said, ending that particular part of the conversation. "Any chance you can give me a ride?"

"Sure," said Crystal. I could see that she wanted to go deeper into Griffin's and my relationship woes, but she also knew better than to push me when I was in this kind of mood.

The strip club was strangely quiet when we got there. The police tape was still up and the place had the air of being almost deserted. Of course, almost deserted didn't mean completely deserted. There, leaning against my car was Detective Liza Ramos.

"You okay?" Crystal asked as she pulled up.

"I'll be fine," I murmured. "I'll talk to you later."

Walking up to Ramos, as usual I was struck by how stunning she was. Thanks to Griffin I also knew that she was a really good cop. She was also not overly fond of me.

"What have I done now?" I asked.

Ramos smiled. "You mean other than setting a self-destruct on your own relationship."

I winced. That hurt, but then I knew Ramos would go for the jugular.

"Any reason you are leaning against my car or did you run out of real criminals to torture?" I asked.

"Last night you told us that there were hidden cameras all through this place. I need you to show me where they are."

"I think Hugh, the cameraman, would be a better person to ask about that," I said, pulling out the keys to my car and starting towards the driver's side.

"I would, but unfortunately it seems the cameraman doesn't have the world's greatest stomach. After he saw Hammy last night he went on a bender. He's pretty hungover at the moment and, to be perfectly honest, doesn't smell the best. I wasn't looking forward to having him in my car. So you're my second choice."

Well, didn't I feel special? Especially since her partner was nowhere to be seen.

"Fine," I said.

The sooner I got this done, the happier I was going to be. I had been in the club before when there was nobody there. I had helped Hugh with the setup of the cameras when we first started this project. Showing Ramos the layout of the hidden cameras, I could see her distaste.

"Did any of the patrons know that they were being taped?" she asked as I showed her a camera that took in the entire first row around the stage.

"As far as I know they weren't notified," I said.

"Alistair has this whole undercover filming reputation that he says gives the real essence of humanity."

"I see a lot of criminals who do the same thing," Ramos said.

"Unfortunately they don't have filmmaking awards on their shelf," I said. "According to society that is what separates art from criminal behavior."

"Don't sound like you're too fond of what is happening here," said Ramos.

"Alistair may have pretensions about what he is doing here," I said. "But the reality is, it is exploitative. These girls have a hard enough job without some jerk who thinks he is better than them, coming in and using their lives to win his next award."

"So, not a fan," Ramos ventured.

"I am very rarely a fan of the people I work with," I said cynically.

"Yet you are still doing it," said Ramos.

"The people you deal with aren't that great either," I reminded her.

Ramos laughed. "That's the truth."

Showing Ramos the area with the workout poles, she eyed me speculatively. "So this is where you were practicing?" she said.

"Yes, and before you ask, no, I am not giving out a demonstration."

"Wasn't going to ask," Ramos said innocently. "Are there cameras in here?"

"Unfortunately yes," I said.

"So you're telling me there is footage of you swinging on this pole." Ramos looked a little too happy at that prospect.

"Number one, despite a great deal of practice, I never got to the swinging level of competency. I was more in the trying to heft myself up and requiring some assistance level. Number two, before a few of us would practice we would stick something over the camera to stop it from taping us."

"Like what?" asked Ramos.

"Depended on where the camera was. If it was poking out between something we would put some fabric from one of the costumes over it. Sometimes I'd cover the lens with duct tape."

"Just as a question, wouldn't that be going against what your boss wants?"

"You really think I do everything my boss wants?" I said. "I spent most of my time listening to women who wanted to completely remove his manhood. I was hosing down fires all the time. In those circumstances, a little bit of obvious rebellion is sometimes required to keep the peace."

Ramos looked confused.

"Alistair was as popular as Hammy with the girls. The fact that it was Hammy and not Alistair with a whip around his throat is pure chance. No one wanted Alistair here, but thanks to Hammy's desperate need for money, they had to put up with him or leave. Not many of them are in a position where they can just walk. My job was to minimize the antagonism towards Alistair. Sometimes I listened to them vent about the creative things they would like to do to him. Other times I fermented a small bit of rebellion. It didn't make any difference to the finished product and it gave everyone some breathing space."

Ramos shook her head. "I really do not understand why you do this job," she said. "At least I've got the option of arresting the people who annoy me."

"Obviously not always," I said. "You still haven't arrested me and I am betting that there has been many a time when you have been sorely tempted."

"Isn't that the truth," sighed Ramos, but she was smiling. I was going to put that into the win column.

Back in the hallway, Ramos noted me frowning. "What's wrong?" she asked.

"There aren't any cameras which are facing the alcove,"

I said.

"I know," said Ramos. "It was one of the first questions we asked the cameraman. Unfortunately easy cases like that do not usually go our way."

"That statue," I said, gesturing towards the truly horrendous piece of artwork that Hammy had pointed out to me on the first day I worked at the club. It was a plaster mold that Hammy had commissioned of himself with a dancer wrapped around him. According to Hammy it was a work of art. I thought it reflected his personality perfectly, cheap and nasty.

Going by the look of distaste on Ramos's face, she agreed with my opinion.

"It shouldn't be here," I said.

"What does it matter if somebody moved it?" she asked.

"It matters because whoever moved it put it directly in front of the only camera which gives a view into the area heading towards the alcove," I said. "You might not be able to get vision of the alcove itself but it would have let you know whether anyone was in the general area."

"You are telling me that the only camera which covers this area was blocked by that monstrosity?" Ramos looked as if she couldn't believe it.

I nodded. "I didn't notice it at first because we constantly move it around. It is so horrendous that Hugh and I made sure it wasn't in any of the footage. We figured no audience should be subjected to an image that raw, regardless of what Alistair believes."

"Which means that whoever killed Hammy knew the camera was here and knew that it was the only one. This wasn't a crime committed on the spur of the moment. There looks like there has been some planning to this one," Ramos said thoughtfully. "How many people knew where the cameras were?"

I shrugged. "Pretty much everyone who worked here. The patrons had no idea about the filming but staff were all completely aware. Most of them had been interviewed at some point, and Alistair, Hugh and I were hardly discreet in what we were doing. Alistair was more interested in the customers anyway."

"We're going to need to get hold of that footage."

"You'll have to speak to Hugh. He's a tech genius and he has all these cameras connected to a wireless network. As far as I know, each of the cameras was uploading elsewhere and he will have all the footage."

"Anything else you can tell me about the two weeks you worked here?" asked Ramos as we walked to our cars.

"I think we've pretty much hit the highlights. I really don't envy you trying to find out who killed the man. I have a feeling there is going to be a very long list."

"The LAPD thanks you for your assistance," said Ramos, smiling.

I chose to ignore the sarcasm.

Chapter Five

To stay true to his gritty reputation, Alistair had his offices in an industrial area of Los Angeles. It was, in effect, a large warehouse with just one office. The rest was an open area which had been decorated with what I would describe as squatting chic. Nothing looked permanent and the term ergonomic was completely disregarded. I found Hugh hard at work on his computer. He looked up when I entered.

"Hey," he muttered.

I took into account the bleary eyes and unshaved face.

"Heard you aren't doing too well this morning." I dropped my purse on my desk and the noise echoed through the large warehouse.

Hugh winced. "Yeah, had a few to drink last night. How did you know?"

"I just had to do a walk through of the club with the cops to show them where all the cameras were."

"Thanks for that," Hugh said. "Wasn't really feeling up to it. Wish I had been though. That cop was…."

"Yeah, hot, I know," I supplied.

Hugh looked at me shrewdly. "Know her do you?"

"Yeah, she's my…" I stopped for a moment. I could say boyfriend's partner but at the moment I wasn't really feeling the whole boyfriend vibe from him. "Friend," I said, wondering how much of the truth I had stretched with that particular statement.

Hugh looked at me curiously. "You don't sound particularly sure about that."

"We have a complicated relationship," I said as I sat down in my chair. "I'm pretty sure she doesn't completely hate me." Of course I could be overestimating the progress Ramos and I had made in our relationship this morning. "What's happening in there?" I asked, indicating Alistair's office.

I could hear the rumble of voices coming through the walls. Usually that wouldn't indicate anything, but that office had been built with blocks that were insanely thick and usually the place was pretty soundproof. For voices to be heard in the main area, even muffled as they were, someone was speaking at a very elevated level.

"One of the girls from the club came to see Alistair." Hugh turned back to his computer.

"Why would they be coming to see Alistair?" I asked.

Hugh looked up and raised an eyebrow with a knowing look.

Oh, that was why. I had a feeling Alistair had been a little less than discreet with some of the women at the club. I hadn't actually seen anything untoward happening, but I had just got one of those feelings.

The door to Alistair's office had come open and Amber walked out, holding herself stiffly and not making eye contact with either Hugh or I as she walked past us.

"Trudie, get in here," barked Alistair from inside his office. I saw Amber flinch.

"Yes," I said shortly as I walked in to find him sitting behind his desk. I could see what Amber saw in Alistair. He was a successful, good looking man. He had the artful messiness of a surfer and it helped him disarm people on those rare occasions when he chose to use charm, rather than his usual personality.

"Deal with her," he said shortly.

"Deal with what?" I asked.

"Amber, just fix her," he growled.

I headed out of the office before I said anything stupid or honest. I found Amber in the parking lot with that look on her face that suggested she was contemplating slashing the tires on Alistair's car.

"Would you like a coffee?" I asked tentatively.

She swung around and I could see the tears that she

was fighting to hide.

"No, I think I should just go home. It was a mistake to come here. I just…I thought he was different. I'm such an idiot. I should have known better."

"Look, I'll buy you a coffee. You can just sit and be quiet for a little bit and decide what you want to do next." I smiled encouragingly and, after a short hesitation, Amber nodded slowly.

Sitting in a booth at a diner in the warehouse district, I had a good look at Amber. Without the dominatrix outfit and the stripper persona I could tell she was a bit older than I had originally thought. Her blonde hair tumbled around her face. She had the fresh faced prettiness that you could see in any number of young girls who came to LA. There was a hardness there as well.

"How long have you been in LA?" I asked.

"I was born here," Amber said, keeping her eyes on the mug of coffee she was holding.

"Do you have family?" I asked.

She nodded.

"Do you want me to call any of them for you?"

Amber shook her head emphatically. Unfortunately I had got that response from a lot of the girls when we had discussed any family they might have.

"Do you want to talk about it?" I asked.

Amber finally looked up at me. "Lots of guys come in to the club looking at picking up strippers. It's kind of a thing they can show off to their buddies about. You learn to just not get involved because it always ends with some form of humiliation. It's like they forget that we're actually women. Alistair just talked to me. I honestly thought he was different. I should have known better. I'm just so stupid."

"You're not stupid. Just because Alistair is being a jerk, it isn't on you. Trust me, that damage was done way before you came on the scene. It has nothing to do with you so don't think for a moment that it does," I said. "Believe me when I say you can do better, I mean you can really do better."

I knew I was being emphatic but if Alistair ever got his head out of his butt long enough for him to find a woman to commit to long term, I was going to have to send flowers, because that was a position that I really did not wish on anybody. Amber shrugged and I could tell she was not convinced. A sudden thought struck me.

"Did Alistair talk to you about what this film would do for you?" I asked.

"He said that the second producers got a look at me on the screen, with what he could do, that I would be knocking back acting jobs. He said I was a natural."

I had to fight the instinct to get out of the booth, find Alistair and kick him hard. Anyone who thinks the casting couch no longer exists in Hollywood is completely deluded. While there were young people desperate for a chance at stardom, there would always be someone eager to take advantage of them. It looked like Alistair had played upon Amber's dream of getting away from the club and into a better life.

"What are you going to do now?" I asked quietly

"Go back to the club, keep working until I can get out I guess." Amber shrugged and I couldn't help feeling sorry for the way her shoulders slumped.

"With Hammy dead, the club could be closing permanently." I hoped I was being gentle enough.

"Hammy's wife is going to take over. As far as I know she plans to open it in a day or two and keep right on going," Amber said.

I choked on my coffee. "Hammy had a wife?" How was that possible? No man who treated women like that should be allowed to marry. There had to be a rule.

"They've been married forever, but I think they were separated," said Amber. "Far as I know, Hammy hadn't seen his wife for years. The cops notified her of the death last night."

"How do you know this?" I asked.

"She got hold of the roster of the girls and has been calling us to make sure we don't move on to other clubs before she can open up again." Amber shrugged again.

I had to admit, I admired the business acumen Hammy's wife had. No point in letting the unsavory murder of your husband get in the way of running a business.

"So are you planning to stay at the club?" I asked.

"I don't have much choice now, do I?" said Amber despondently.

Chapter Six

Back at the office I thought about what Amber had said. Finding Alistair standing behind Hugh as they ran through some footage, I marveled at his complete lack of awareness that the way he treated people was wrong.

"Did you know that Hammy was married?" I asked Alistair as I sat down.

"To a woman?" asked Alistair.

"I believe so," I said. "Seems she's taking over the club now that Hammy is no longer with us."

Alistair's brow furrowed. "I need more time with this shoot. I'm going to have to speak to her to see if she'll extend the contract that we had with Hammy."

Even before I came back to the office I knew what he would want. A part of me hated the fact that I was right and even worse that I was prepared.

"I have her details here if you want to get in touch with her."

Alistair clapped his hands together. "This is why you are the best assistant I've ever had. At first glance you didn't look like much but you have a brain and you use it. I must say, originally, I didn't have high hopes but you've really surprised me. Contact the woman and see about our permissions to continue filming."

After he walked back into his office I turned to Hugh. "He just insulted me along with that compliment didn't he?"

Hugh nodded.

"There are seminars where they teach that skill to guys who are desperate to pick up women don't they?"

Hugh nodded again, keeping his eyes firmly on the screen in front of him.

"When did the world get so messed up?" I asked.

Hugh didn't bother to answer what was obviously a rhetorical question.

I was still thinking that as I stood at the door of Denise Pollard. Why was I having to approach this woman, less than twenty-four hours after the death of her husband, to get permission to continue filming in the strip club that she was taking over?

When the door opened I could feel my eyes widen in surprise. Whatever I had expected from Hammy Pollard's wife, this was not it. Denise Pollard looked like my grandmother. She looked much older than I was expecting. Her hair was an iron gray and was scraped back severely from her face. Her eyes were a brilliant blue and I could see the spark of intelligence in them. She was a large woman and the shapeless dress she wore did nothing to hide that.

"What can I do for you?" she asked a little tentatively, obviously concerned by the stranger knocking at her door.

I rushed to reassure her. "Mrs Pollard, my name is Trudie Eyre. I was working at your husband's club."

Denise raked me from head to toe and she frowned. "I'm sorry, I didn't see your name on the employee list. You don't look like someone who would work at Hammy's."

I was undecided whether that statement was a compliment or not.

"No," I said quickly. "I didn't work for Hammy. I'm not sure if one of the other girls told you but Hammy was working on a project with the filmmaker, Alistair Hopkins."

Denise nodded. "One of the girls did mention it but I have to tell you, I've had a lot to deal with today. I really hadn't even thought about that kind of thing."

I smiled, hoping to appear non-threatening. "I was wondering if I would be able to come in and have a talk with you. Alistair is very keen to continue his project at the club and we were hoping we would be able to come to some accommodation."

Denise Pollard studied me for a moment. She opened the door wider to let me in and I stepped through.

"I'm sorry if I seem inhospitable," she said as she led me down the hallway. "I've learned to be suspicious of people. It's not an easy habit to break."

"It's smart to be wary," I said.

"I was just putting on some tea," Denise said. "Would you like some?"

"I'd love it, thank you." I smiled at the way Denise reminded me of my Grandma Rita.

"Just take a seat in here," she said, indicating the main room. "I'll be right out."

I stepped into the living room and was surprised at the large piano that dominated the space. On top of the piano I found photos in frames. I found one with Denise when she was young, standing next to a much younger version of Hammy Pollard, in a white mini dress.

"Our wedding day," Denise said sadly from behind me.

"I'm sorry," I said, as I put the photo back. "I didn't mean to pry."

She handed me a cup of tea. "It was a long time ago." She pulled out another photo. "This one is when I used to work at Hammy's club."

I took the photo and looked at it. In it was Denise in one of the skimpy costumes that I had become used to seeing on the dancers at the club. She was posed on a pole, her strength and flexibility obvious to see. I could see why Hammy had been taken with her. In her younger days Denise had been beautiful.

Glancing up at Denise, I saw her frown as she patted her hair. "Time has not been kind to me. That photo was taken a lifetime ago."

I put the photo down and took a sip of tea.

"How did you meet Hammy?" I asked.

"Would you believe at church?" Denise said.

I stopped myself from choking on the tea. I had to admit that the thought of Hammy Pollard in a church was a bit of a stretch.

"His mother was still alive back then. He doted on that woman. She never knew that he owned a strip club. He managed to keep it from her and convinced her that he was an accountant. He even did her taxes for her. How she didn't fall foul of the IRS is a miracle to me, because he had no idea what he was doing, but his mother had to believe it. I was new in LA, wanting to be an actress of course, like every young girl who came here. I went to church, because that was how I was raised, and I met Hammy. I didn't know what he did at first, but when my big break didn't come and I was running out of money, he came to me with an offer. He thought I had the right look to be one of his girls. He timed it perfectly. I trusted him and I'd reached the point where I was desperate. Before I knew what was happening I was on stage. Soon after I was the headline act. I thought Hammy was in love with me and I was devoted to him. He swept me off my feet and proposed. I found out later that he only married me because his mother was dying and it was her final wish that he be married before she died. After she died I was considered surplus to requirements. He left me six months later."

"I'm sorry," I said awkwardly.

"Don't be," she said. "Everything works out for a reason. I stopped working at the club. I was fortunate and got a job at the church. It gave me a purpose."

"You never divorced Hammy?" I ventured.

Denise shook her head. "No, Hammy didn't believe in divorce and like he said, he was never going to marry again. Having a wife gave him a ready excuse if any of the girls got a bit clingy."

Hammy really had been a prince among men. The more I knew about him, the more surprised I was that somebody hadn't killed him years ago.

44

"So you are now the owner of the club. Why would Hammy leave it to you?"

Denise smiled. "There was no one else to leave it to. Hammy always said that he would change his will if there was someone he cared about enough to change it for. It looks like he never found anyone."

"Is there any reason why you aren't going to sell it immediately?" I asked.

There must have been a strange look on my face because Denise smiled at me. "I have not had an easy time since Hammy left me. This may be my one and only chance to make something out of my life. I worked in the bar, I know how it was run. Despite what Hammy believed about all his girls, I was a lot smarter than he thought I was. I know Hammy had pretty much run the place into the ground. I think I can build it up again."

I was impressed. She may not look like I imagined a strip club owner would look, but she was determined.

"Some of the girls have told me about the man you work for," Denise said thoughtfully.

I had to stop myself from cringing. Nothing that those girls had said about Alistair was going to be in his favor.

"The girls are not particularly fond of him," said Denise.

That was a mild way of putting it.

"But he brings money to the table," she mused.

I nodded, letting her go ahead with her one sided negotiation.

"I think that I will let him continue with his filming, temporarily," Denise continued. "However, I will be watching very carefully. If I find that he is in any way acting inappropriately with my girls, I will be forced to reevaluate my stance."

I nodded again. "Thank you," I said as I held out my hand.

She grasped it strongly. I could see the excitement in her eyes. She looked like someone who had found a project and was going to grasp hold of it with both hands. I had a feeling that Alistair wasn't going to know what hit him.

Chapter Seven

After giving Denise, Alistair's card and extracting a promise that as soon as the police gave her control of the club, she would contact us, I realized that I hadn't had a chance to eat and swung into a diner. As I sat down in a booth my phone rang.

"Trudie, where are you?" barked Alistair.

"I'm grabbing something to eat," I said. "I've spoken to Denise Pollard and she has agreed to temporarily allow you to continue filming, as long as there aren't any unfavorable incidents with the girls."

"That's good, very good," said Alistair in that rushed way he had of speaking. After working for him for a month I was very much aware that the only words he heard me say was 'continue filming'. I could see I was going to be busy trying to keep Alistair and Denise from rubbing each other the wrong way.

"I have meetings with that new lawyer of mine all afternoon. He has just gone through the proposal for this shoot and he is concerned about some of the legal ramifications."

Color me surprised. The lawyer was concerned that there may be legal fallout from videotaping men in a strip bar without their knowledge. I did not see that coming.

"I need you to finish transcribing some of the footage as well as my notes," Alistair said. "Hugh has gone home so the office is closed for the day. You can work from home and I expect that transcribing to be done immediately."

After being given my orders I tucked my phone in my bag. I did not see this job going well. It seemed to be unraveling. There was a part of me that hoped that

Alistair's new lawyer was so horrified by the project that he would bury it under piles of paperwork.

My plate of food was placed in front of me and I looked up to thank the waitress, only to be faced with my own special brand of torment.

Dominic Caldwell slid into the booth opposite me and gave me that smile that only he seemed to be able to do. A smile which brought to mind a combination of innocent puppy dog in pet shop window and alligator just before attacking its prey and dragging it into the swamp. I looked around desperately, evaluating the exits and how soon I could get through them, into my car and out of the state.

"Don't panic," Dominic murmured. "You're perfectly safe."

I think I was going to take that statement with a pinch of salt. Dominic Caldwell had, during a previous encounter, kidnapped me. Twice. For most people that kind of background to a relationship might lead you to expect it to be strained. Dominic was not most people. For some reason he thought we had bonded. The thinking processes of some people absolutely amazed me. He confused me and frankly he scared me. If Griffin was mad at me for being friends with Travis, he was going to be apoplectic when he discovered that I was having lunch with Dominic. Because he would find out, that was just the way that my life was going.

"What are you doing here?" I croaked.

"I thought it would be useful for us to have a conversation," Dominic said. "But please, eat your lunch. I wouldn't want it to get cold."

I looked down at the burger and fries sitting on the plate. They seemed a lot more appetizing when I ordered them. Of course, that was before they were delivered by my own personal spawn of Satan. Admittedly I may have been exaggerating the perceived evil of the man sitting across from me. The problem was that Dominic Caldwell both scared and unsettled me. I firmly believed in the benefits of civilization. Everybody is supposed to work within the rules of the law. Dominic has his own interpretation of what those laws are and how they apply to him. Usually they don't. I had been made acutely aware of this when I found myself arguing the strict definition of what a kidnapping actually was.

I picked up the burger and took a bite out of it. If I was going to be kidnapped again I may as well have it happen when I had a full stomach.

Dominic watched me quietly as I ate the burger. The silence seemed to stretch out uncomfortably and I could feel my entire body tensing up.

Finishing the burger, I wiped my hands with the napkin and sat back.

"What do you want, Dominic?" I was pleased that my voice didn't shake.

"Just a chat," said Dominic. "I have so missed our chats."

I hadn't. I was quite happy with a life that did not include chats with Dominic Caldwell.

"What exactly did you want to chat about?" I asked. "I wouldn't have believed my thoughts on any topic would be relevant to you."

"Oh, Trudie," said Dominic. "I thought I had made myself clear that I treasure the time we have together. I find your insights into certain matters to be invaluable."

"And what insights are you looking for at the moment?" I asked, because there was no way that I was ever going to believe that this meeting between the two of us was coincidental. Even I'm not that unlucky.

Dominic sighed. "I believe that you found Hamish Pollard's body."

I nodded, wondering why that would mean anything to Dominic.

"Mr Pollard and I had a business relationship."

"What kind of business relationship?" I asked.

"Mr Pollard was a frequent customer at several of my

establishments" said Dominic.

That explained it. From what little I knew about Dominic, he owned several casinos in Las Vegas. Considering the level of interest shown in him by both local and federal law enforcement agencies, I am sure there was far more to his empire but I was only aware of this small area.

"I'm guessing he owed you money," I said.

"As usual your insight astounds me," said Dominic.

I was confused. "What are you doing here, Dominic?" I asked. "Whatever Hammy owed you could not possibly be worth you coming to LA yourself and chasing up the money."

Dominic smiled. "You are correct or course. I would usually not be dealing with this issue myself but I heard of your involvement and it did pique my interest."

I did not want to pique his interest. I had never wanted to pique his interest. Dominic Caldwell was a handsome, rich and powerful man, but he had a way of doing business which was slightly left of completely legal. All of a sudden I had a very frightening thought.

"You haven't sent one of your colleagues to talk to Denise Pollard have you?" I asked, the dismay obvious in my voice. I had met two of Dominic's colleagues. The first one stuck a needle in my neck, rendering me unconscious for nine hours. The second kidnapped me from a drugstore. I started to get out of the booth.

Dominic placed a hand over mine on the table, effectively trapping me in place.

"Where do you think you are going?" he asked quietly.

"I'm going to rescue Denise from whatever thug you sent after her."

"Mrs Pollard is in safe hands. My colleague has been informed that he is to treat her with the utmost respect. My instructions were made very clear in this regard," Dominic said.

I stayed standing. "I don't have the greatest confidence

in your communication skills."

Dominic smiled. "I do like you."

I wasn't particularly fond of that sentiment either.

"Trust me," he said, indicating that I should sit down again.

I almost choked on those words. I was as likely to trust Dominic Caldwell as I was a politician's promises. Dominic obviously knew where my thought processes were going and I saw his features tighten.

"I would suggest you accept my word in this," he said grimly.

I sat down because I could tell that I didn't really have a choice.

"Why are you here?" I asked, pulling my hand back from where he was still holding it.

He let go grudgingly. "Mr Pollard's death is quite inconvenient. We had been discussing a possible business relationship."

I couldn't help the look of distaste that crossed my face. "You were looking into owning strip clubs?" I know that Dominic Caldwell was many things but I hadn't realized that he was involved in that industry.

Dominic's face matched mine. "Of course not, but that land that the club sits on is quite valuable. Mr Pollard owed me a considerable amount of money and he was considering providing me with the land as compensation."

"For what?" I asked.

"For development. I am an honest businessman and I saw an opportunity to expand into certain areas of Los Angeles. I have found lately that this city holds some attraction," Dominic said to me, his gaze holding mine.

I swallowed. Dominic Caldwell made me nervous, very nervous.

"Why do you want to talk to me?" I asked, keeping my voice low.

"Having Mr Pollard pass away like he did, at such an important part of the negotiations, I find that concerning.

I am curious as to what happened."

"Why are you asking me?" I said. "Why don't you just go to the police, or a private investigator, or anyone else but me."

Yet again Dominic looked at me as if he was having to explain things to a child. "I just want to know what you saw and any thoughts you may have regarding Mr Pollard's unfortunate demise."

I truly had to stop myself from sighing in exasperation. "I don't know anything. I was one of the people who found the body last night. I've been working at the club for the last couple of weeks. During that time I have found Hammy to be a thoroughly disgusting human being. The fact he was murdered does not surprise me at all. He was strangled with a whip that was used in the dominatrix's act. I have absolutely no idea who did this. If you are looking for the killer, the list could be a mile long."

"Your boyfriend has no problem with you working in a strip club?" Dominic asked in what I felt was a totally unrelated question.

"It's not like I was stripping," I said tightly, refusing to answer the question.

Dominic studied me carefully. "He didn't know, did he?"

"I am pretty sure that my personal life is none of your business," I said. "In fact, there is no part of my life that is any of your business. If you have issues with Hammy or if he owed you money then I would suggest that you sort it out with his estate."

"That is the thing," said Dominic, as usual completely ignoring the fact that I very obviously wanted to get away from him. "The wife with the old will, it seems a little too convenient. It was my understanding that Mr Pollard had developed a relationship with a young lady recently and had been planning to change his will to leave her the club if something unfortunate happened to him."

"Really?" I said and wanted to kick myself.

Unfortunately, Dominic knew that I had an insatiable curiosity. Already my mind was racing, trying to work out who the young lady in question could have been. I was assuming that it was one of the girls from the club but maybe Hammy had a hobby that I didn't know about. People sometimes have a habit of surprising you. For all I knew, Hammy could have belonged to a book club. I was doubting it, but I'd been completely wrong about people before.

"I prefer to ascertain as much as I can about a situation before making my next move," said Dominic. He pulled a card out of his pocket and pushed it across the table towards me. "My understanding is that you are continuing to work at the club. I would be very appreciative if you were to contact me if any further information should come your way."

I reluctantly picked up his card and looked at it carefully. I knew I was being paranoid but a part of me was concerned that there could be a tracking device embedded in it. Based on what I knew about Dominic Caldwell, I wouldn't be surprised.

Turning over the card I looked up at him. "Why me?" I asked. "There are so many ways that you can find out the information that you want. Why did you come to me?"

Dominic smiled. "It is true that I am following other lines of inquiry. Getting this land is important to me. Still, I find I value your insights into these matters. You have a refreshing way of looking at life. If you were available I would be interested in offering you a position on my staff."

For a moment I forgot to breathe. I was being head hunted by a man who, depending on which rumor you listened to, may or may not perform that activity literally.

"Thank you," I said, remembering to breathe again, although I did find that my voice was pitched a little high. "At this time I don't think that I am looking for another position. I'm quite happy where I am."

Dominic stood up, picked up my hand and brushed a gentle kiss across the back of my knuckles. "Until we meet again," he said.

I started breathing again when he walked out of the door of the diner.

Chapter Eight

Closing the door to my apartment, I leaned back against it and closed my eyes. Here I felt safe.

"Did you want to tell me what you've been doing?"

My eyes flew open and I stopped a scream when I saw it was Griffin.

"What are you doing here?" I was smiling. I couldn't help it. Griffin had come back. We were going to discuss our issues like adults and sort them out. Our relationship would survive and we would come out of this stronger. Griffin would realize how much he loved me and everything would be perfect.

"You were having lunch with Dominic Caldwell," Griffin accused.

I raised my eyes to the heavens. I could not catch a break. "How on Earth did you know that? I only left him about twenty minutes ago."

"Take your pick," said Griffin. "There is more than one law enforcement agency keeping an eye on the guy and when he sits down to lunch with my girlfriend, I start getting phone calls."

At least that was one question for the day answered, Griffin still considered that I was his girlfriend.

"I was sitting in a diner having lunch when he came up to speak to me. It seems that Hammy owed him some money, because that is the way my life goes. He wondered if I had any ideas who could have possibly killed Hammy."

"And he was asking you because..."

"Because for some reason the man values my opinion."

Griffin looked at me skeptically. I was with him. Dominic Caldwell's unswerving confidence in my powers of observation and deduction caused me to question the man's grasp on reality.

"Are there any other men that I should be worried about you keeping company with?" asked Griffin. "I mean in twenty-four hours I find you spending time in a strip club with Cooper and then having a friendly lunch with Dominic Caldwell."

Just like that my dreams of a mature discussion and loving reconciliation went out of the window.

"It wasn't my fault," I said, wondering if I was overusing that phrase. "Dominic came and spoke to me about Hammy's death. He was in the middle of buying the land that the club is on in repayment for some debts Hammy had with him. According to Dominic, the death happened at an unfortunate time during the negotiations." I grimaced a bit. That sounded a little bit too much like something Dominic would say. I was beginning to sound like him. I was going to have to nip that in the bud pretty quickly.

"Really," said Griffin as he pulled out his phone. "And at which part of the discussion did he feel the need to kiss you?"

"What are you talking about?" I really couldn't believe the way this conversation was going.

Griffin showed me the screen on his phone and there was a lovely photo of Dominic kissing my hand. Obviously one of those law enforcement agencies had felt that Griffin needed that bit of information as well. Good to see my tax dollars at work. Now that I thought about it, I wouldn't put it past Dominic to have known we were being watched. It would appeal to his sense of humor to put me in this position.

"He was leaving and I thought he was shaking my hand when he kissed it lightly. You're the one always telling me how dangerous he is. Did you want me to just haul off and slap him?" I said.

I could tell that there were two parts of Griffin warring against each other. The side that wanted me to hit the man who dared to touch me and the side that knew how bad a move that would have been.

"You have to stop stepping into these situations," Griffin said tightly.

"What are you talking about?" I replied.

"Finding bodies, dealing with people who are dangerous. You just don't think about the consequences of what you are doing," Griffin said as he started pacing the room.

"None of this is my fault," I said. I was getting tired of having to constantly tell people this.

"Yet you are always in the middle of it," Griffin said.

I stopped. Maybe he was right. There had to be some reason why I found myself in these situations. I'd spent my whole life being the good, responsible, practical girl. Was it possible that I was actually a trouble magnet who attracted the bad boys? I mean, Dominic definitely fell under that definition, but I preferred to think of Travis as more slightly off track rather than completely bad. Maybe I was giving out some weird psychic vibes that attracted trouble. Seriously, I was working in a strip club for a man who thought it was completely acceptable to film people without their knowledge. How could that possibly come under the banner of being normal? Maybe I should talk to Monique about getting me a nice quiet office job for a change. No celebrities, no eccentric artists, just me, a computer and a few weeks without dealing with the insanity that was Hollywood.

"You've got to start thinking before you rush into these messes, Trudie, or one day you're going to get hurt." Griffin kept going, not realizing that he was now talking to himself. I was having the beginning of a life crisis over in my part of the room.

"Are you even listening to me?" he asked as he stopped pacing.

No I wasn't. I nodded though, no point in getting him madder than he already was. Unfortunately, Griffin knew me better than that and he knew that I had checked out of this conversation several minutes ago. He stiffened noticeably. "If you're not interested in what I have to say then I guess I'd better just go."

"Don't, Jake, please." I hated when Griffin and I argued. "Can't we just sit down and talk about this, try to sort it out before it gets to the point we can't fix it."

I thought I'd got through to him, but then the shutters came over his emotions and that blank shell that he was famed for in the police force came back. "I need to get back to work," he said.

I stepped aside from the door. "Fine." I wasn't going to stop him. If he wasn't ready to fight for us then I wasn't going to try to force him. Griffin opened the door only to find Sean standing outside, hand raised, ready to knock. He nodded at Sean and stalked off.

Sean followed Griffin with his eyes and then swung around to me.

"Griffin looked mad," said Sean.

"Just a little disagreement," I said.

"What did you do?" asked Sean.

I turned my head to him slowly, trying desperately to remember that he was a teenage boy and sometimes he walked into areas where he had no business being.

"What do you mean, what did I do?" I said softly.

Of course, and I blamed his youth for this, Sean didn't see the warning signs. He unfortunately also had a bit of hero worship when it came to Griffin and thought he could do no wrong.

"You must have done something wrong for Griffin to be so mad with you."

"Sean," I said, with all the patience of someone who had a teenage brother. Sean had been kicked out by his mother and had ended up living in the apartment block with the owner, Miss Betsy and I keeping an eye on him. I didn't want to upset him but he needed to know the boundaries. "My relationship with Griffin is none of your business. Believe me when I say you do not want to wander into the middle of it."

Sean turned around and walked away, but not before I had seen the hurt on his face.

"Sean, wait," I said as he stalked off.

He didn't bother to turn around. Wonderful. Another man in my life was now mad at me. I seemed to be batting a thousand these days.

Chapter Nine

For the rest of the day I threw myself into my work. One thing I liked about my job was that I was able to use it to forget the way the rest of my life was slowly unravelling. That was a skill I was really grateful for. By the time I finished work it was late and it hit me that Griffin hadn't bothered to call me. While we'd been together, even when he was busy with a murder, I'd usually get at least a text. At the moment my cell was silent. I think that more than anything brought home to me the problems we were having. If he didn't trust me there wasn't much I could do about it. I wasn't going to spend my life not talking to men just because my boyfriend didn't seem to be able to handle it. Of course, with Dominic Caldwell I would make an exception. I would be quite happy never to speak to that man again in my life.

As usual I was woken up by my cell ringing on my bedside table. For the millionth time I swore that I would turn it off before going to sleep.

"What?" I croaked.

"I need you to go to the club and deliver some papers for Pollard's wife to sign," barked Alistair.

"What?" I repeated.

Alistair sighed. I could tell he was annoyed that I wanted an explanation, but he was the inconsiderate one who was calling me at the crack of dawn, so as far as I was concerned he could show me at least a bit of courtesy.

"Denise Pollard is opening the bar up tonight. My lawyer is insisting that I get additional paperwork signed by the new owner. When I tried to speak to her she took something I said the wrong way. I need you to fix it and get her to sign the papers. I'm at the office so you can swing by here first." Alistair finished and I'm sure he was congratulating himself on how patient he was being with his numbskull assistant who didn't snap to consciousness immediately when he called.

"Fine," I said and hung up.

Rather than rushing to Alistair's bidding, I took the time to make myself a coffee. Considering how the day had started, I had a very good feeling that I was going to need it.

"What took you so long?" snapped Alistair when I made it to the office.

I was right. I was definitely glad I'd stopped for a coffee. I didn't even bother to reply. I just held out my hand for the paperwork. That movement obviously annoyed Alistair because I could see his face going red. He shoved the papers in my direction and I turned around and walked out. I berated myself when I got in the car. Usually I handled situations like that with tact and diplomacy. Today I really didn't feel like it. I was missing Griffin. I was used to not seeing him for days on end. It was the nature of the police business. When there was a case, that took his attention. I understood that. What I didn't like was the fact that I knew I wouldn't even be getting his short, sharp text messages. They might not have said much but at least they let me know that he thought of me.

The club was quiet when I got there. It was early morning and when I took the time to think about it and not just react to Alistair's orders, I realized that maybe I should have contacted Denise before turning up. I went around the back to the staff entrance and was surprised to see it open.

"Hello," I called out as I walked through the back rooms. Considering my discussion with Griffin, I was beginning to seriously think about walking out. If I was the trouble magnet that everybody seemed to assume I was, then a deserted strip bar was the perfect place for something to go terribly wrong. I heard noises and followed them to the dressing room. There I found Amber with her arm around the shoulders of one of the other girls. I wracked my brain to remember her name. She was a quiet one who stayed in the background and, miraculously, Alistair hadn't yet managed to turn her homicidal so I hadn't really had anything to do with her.

"Sorry," I said as they looked up. "I didn't mean to intrude.

Amber waved me in. "It's not a problem. Brandi's a little upset."

I sat down next to them. "Is there anything I can do to help?" I asked.

"He promised," wailed Brandi as she took in gulps of air between heaving sobs.

Great. I really didn't want to know if Alistair made promises to other girls that he had no intention of fulfilling.

Amber caught my eye and I could see she saw where my assumption had gone.

"No," she murmured. "It wasn't Alistair this time. It was Hammy."

I raised an eyebrow.

"He said he would leave the bar to me. He said he loved me." Brandi continued sobbing.

Amber had the same disbelieving look on her face that I did. I didn't want to point out to the distraught young woman how gullible she had been, but I don't think anyone would seriously believe that he would leave the place to one of the dancers. Denise had given me a firsthand account of how much sensitivity Hammy showed towards women.

Brandi was a pretty little thing and I could see how she appealed to Hammy. From what I recalled, she was friendly enough but not as out there as some of the other girls. It was the reason she hadn't caught Alistair's eye.

"Sometimes men say things they don't mean," I said gently.

"But he showed me the new will. He just needed to get

it signed," Brandi said.

"Has anyone else seen the will?" I asked.

Amber shook her head. "I spoke to Denise yesterday. The only will that was with the lawyer was the one that leaves the place to her. According to the lawyer there was never an updated will."

Brandi continued sobbing. I could understand that she was disappointed but she was beginning to give me a headache.

"Maybe you should go clean yourself up," I said, slightly concerned that I had seemed to lose my sense of empathy.

Brandi tottered off to the bathroom on her ankle twisting platform shoes.

"Thanks for that," mumbled Amber. "I didn't think she was ever going to stop crying."

"She might want to stop with the whole changing of the will talk or else people are going to start looking at her as a viable suspect," I said.

"Wouldn't want that," said Amber. "Although it might take the heat off me for a while."

"Have you been having problems?" I asked.

"Unfortunately the murder weapon comes from my act," said Amber. The cops have spoken to me several times about it. Luckily it looks like I was on stage at the same time as Hammy was getting killed."

I looked at her strangely.

"I know it sounds bad when I say it," said Amber, "but when you're searching for an alibi, dancing naked in front of a bunch of men is a pretty good one. Seems my act that night was considered pretty memorable."

"I guess that leaves the wife," I said. "Denise must be having a lot of questions to answer."

Amber shook her head. "Not her either. Seems she was at a church meeting at the time Hammy got killed. Unfortunately for the cops, it looks like the two best suspects have ironclad alibis, one at a church and one on stage at a strip club."

"I didn't realize that Brandi was involved with Hammy," I said, changing the subject.

"Hammy's been involved with a lot of the girls at one time or another," Amber replied.

I looked at her sideways.

"No," she said. "Before you even think of asking, no. I never went there and I never wanted to." She hurriedly changed the subject. "Why are you here so early anyway?"

"It seems the lawyers want Denise to sign some more papers before Alistair can continue with the filming," I said. "Apparently Denise is pretty close to telling Alistair what he can do with his cameras, so I got nominated to speak to her on his behalf."

Amber laughed but I could still see the hurt in her eyes.

"I'm really sorry for how he treated you," I said softly.

"It isn't your fault," said Amber. "It isn't the first time I've had a guy promise me the world and not deliver, and I'm sure it won't be the last. Sometimes I wonder if I shouldn't give up on men altogether. I only seem to be disappointed by them."

I could only nod in sympathy.

I turned as I heard a throat being cleared.

"Sorry to interrupt, ladies," said Denise, "but I was wondering if I could speak to Amber in private."

"Sure," said Amber.

"Did you need something, Trudie?" asked Denise.

"I was just supposed to ask you to sign some paperwork that Alistair's lawyers have sent through," I said.

Denise smiled. "That man may be a lot of things but he isn't dumb. He knew you'd have a better chance of getting me to look at them than he ever would."

I smiled, because really, she was right on the money.

Denise held out her hand and took the papers. "I'll have a look and if they're acceptable I'll get you to come back and get them this afternoon."

"Thanks for that," I said.

On the way out of the club I passed Hugh coming in with some equipment.

"What are you doing?" I asked.

"Just some work with the lighting. Some of the footage isn't coming out as well as we'd like and Alistair's losing his mind over it."

"I haven't got the final paperwork from Denise so she might not let you in," I warned.

Hugh flashed me a grin. "Trust me," he said. "I'll be able to sweet talk my way in."

I gave him an answering smile. I had to admit that I admired the man's confidence.

Chapter Ten

The office was quiet thanks to both Alistair and Hugh being out. I was surprised when the door to the warehouse opened and Lee was standing there.

I smiled. "Lee, what are you doing here?"

Lee's face looked strained. "I know you and Jake are having some problems."

"You can't get in the middle of this, Lee," I warned. "I've told you before that Griffin and I will work things out ourselves."

Lee looked nervous. "I know and believe it or not, I wouldn't be doing this unless I really felt that it was an emergency situation."

I sighed. I knew that look on Lee's face. He was a man on a mission and nothing I said was going to change his mind. The best thing would be for me to let him say his piece.

"Take a seat, Lee. I'll hear you out."

Lee smiled gratefully and sat down on the opposite side of my desk.

"Angela contacted Jake."

I grimaced. With everything else that had been happening, I had managed to push the impending meeting between Griffin and his absent mother out of my mind.

"He is meeting her for lunch today," said Lee.

"What do you want me to do, Lee?" I asked. "Griffin and I aren't exactly on the best terms at the moment. I really don't know if he'd be interested in my interfering with his life."

"I know," said Lee and he abruptly stood up. "I shouldn't have done this. You're right, I should just keep out of it. He's a grown man. He doesn't need his father interfering in his life. I just don't want to see him get hurt."

I got up from my seat and gave him a hug. "You are an amazing dad."

Lee nodded quickly and left but not before I saw the tears in his eyes. I sat down in my chair and thought about the last couple of days. I also thought about Griffin and exactly what I was willing to risk for him.

"Dammit," I yelled to the empty walls and grabbed my purse. I texted Alistair that I would be taking some time off and headed home.

Standing in the street outside the restaurant Lee had told me Griffin was meeting his mother, when I'd called him while getting ready, I hoped that I had made the right decision. I saw Griffin striding along the footpath towards the restaurant. He faltered when he saw me standing at the front of the building.

Griffin walked up to me and I awkwardly fidgeted with my clutch.

"What are you doing here?" he asked.

"Lee told me that you were meeting with your mom. I know that's a big deal for you so I'm here. If you want me with you, I'll go in with you. If you want me to go home, I can do that too. I just wanted you to know that you're not alone in this."

I had no idea how this was going to play out and I had mentally prepared myself for the blow to my pride if he told me he didn't want me there. Despite that preparation, if he sent me away, I wasn't sure if there was enough ice cream in the state to deal with the emotional meltdown I was going to go through.

Griffin studied me. "I've said some pretty rough things to you the last couple of days," he said softly.

I nodded. "Yes you did, and believe me, when this is all sorted out, you and I are going to have some words, but for right now we deal with this, then after we'll discuss what a jerk you've been. Now what do you want me to do?"

Griffin hesitated and I prepared myself for a taste of

humiliating rejection.

"I want you with me," he said, holding out his hand.

"Then I'm with you," I said, grasping his hand with mine, relief coursing through me.

He folded me into his side and put his arm around me.

"You look beautiful," he said softly.

"You can thank the girls at the bar for that," I said tartly. "Swinging on a pole wasn't the only thing they were teaching me. They threw in hair and makeup lessons as well."

Griffin smiled tightly.

"Can you do this?" I asked gently. Most of the time Griffin was one of the strongest men I knew, but the mom issue seemed to be a big one for him.

He shrugged. "The woman wants to meet me. A part of me is curious to see what she is like. I know what she looks like, I've known who she is for a long time now. I just never thought I'd actually meet her. I guess this is the one chance I'll get." He looked down at me. "I know what it took for you to be here, especially the way things have been between us. It means a lot."

I nodded. I didn't know what to say really. Once Lee told me what was happening, I didn't really have a choice. You do what you have to for those you love.

The restaurant was one of those expensive places which is completely wasted on someone like me. I do not have the sophisticated palate required to discern the amount of skill which goes into both the food and the decor. Griffin led me to the table where his mother was waiting for us. She smiled up at him. The smile died when she saw me with him.

"I did not realize you were bringing a guest," she said with a slightly accusing tone.

Griffin shrugged in that way that he had and I smiled apologetically.

Within several moments a third placing was added to the table and Griffin and I were seated. I had to admit I was curious to see how this was going to play out. Was she going to explain why she left Griffin and his father? Was she going to apologize? There was no way this lunch was going to be anything other than awkward.

Angela cleared her throat and you could tell that there was a bit of nervousness there. It seemed so at odds with the cool exterior she presented to the world. "I guess you're wondering why I asked to meet you."

"I do find it curious," said Griffin. "You left my dad thirty years ago and we haven't heard a word from you since and now out of the blue you want to meet me."

Angela smiled ingratiatingly. "I was very young when I married your father. I didn't realize what marriage would entail and having a baby was something that I was really not prepared for. I was frightened by it and your father was no help at all."

Both Griffin and I stiffened at the slight against Lee. I adored Lee and he had raised Griffin on his own the best he could. Lee was the first to admit that his parenting skills may not have been perfect, but he loved his son and did the best by him. As evidenced by the fact that he came down to my office to give me the heads up about this touching family reunion. Angela had made her first mistake by blaming Lee for her choices.

Griffin obviously felt the same way that I did as he moved to interrupt her. "I'm really not interested in why you left. You made your choice then and I don't think we need to revisit it. What I want to know is why you want to see me now."

I thought that Griffin had asked a clear question. From what I could see, Griffin thought he had asked a clear question. Unfortunately Angela's response was to start telling us about her life, from the moment that she walked out of the door leaving Lee and Griffin far behind. For the next hour Griffin and I were subjected to a discussion on the lifestyles of the rich and famous. Lee had told me that Angela had been a socialite trust fund baby but I had never truly grasped what that meant. It was only after we had made our way through lunch and had moved on to drinks that I was able to fully appreciate how wealthy Angela's family was. From what I could tell, her life had been one long vacation party that just moved through various parts of the world. Not once did she ask about her son's life. I marveled at the complete lack of awareness that this woman had regarding her child. Despite the fact that I was concerned about the emotional toll this situation was having on Griffin, he looked completely bored and at one point I had seen him stifle a yawn. When his cell rang he looked so pathetically grateful for the interruption that a part of me wondered if he had set it up with Ramos. He ducked away from the table leaving me with his mother who had barely noticed his absence.

When Griffin came back to the table, for the first time during this meeting, he looked happy.

"I am sorry," he announced, "but work is calling. I have a case to get to."

I started to rise, grateful for the premature end to this torture, only to feel Angela's hand on mine. "That's fine. It will give Trudie and me a chance to get to know each other. I am so looking forward to getting to know the woman who captured my boy's heart."

I froze and, resigned to my fate, I sat down again.

Griffin nodded and leaned over to kiss me on the cheek. "I am so sorry," he whispered in my ear before nodding at his mother and making his getaway.

I gazed longingly at his back as he strode away from us.

"You seem to be very fond of my son," Angela said, mistaking my wistful gaze for me being clingy, as opposed to me wanting to escape with him.

I nodded as I grabbed a glass of water.

"I'm glad to know that he has someone in his life who cares for him." Angela patted me on the hand. "I need to have my son back in my life," she said. "I want you to be a part of it." She smiled at me and I had to control the shiver. That smile was not real. I work with fake, I specialize in fake, and believe me, that smile was fake. Something was going on here and I had a feeling it had nothing to do with a mother realizing that she wanted to have her son back in her life.

I eventually managed to make my escape from Griffin's mother, only after she had extracted a promise for us to have a girl's day so we could get to know each other better. I immediately headed for Monique's office. If anyone was going to know why Angela wanted her son back, it was going to be Monique.

Chapter Eleven

Walking into Monique's office, I shouldn't have been surprised to find my friend and Crystal's husband, Edwin, working on the front desk. Until recently Edwin had been an aspiring actor. Unfortunately he had no talent at all for acting. Some people just didn't. At least he had been brave enough to try. The realization that he wasn't going to make it in the acting world had been hard for Edwin, but he had dealt with it and took as many temporary jobs as he could to fill in, until he found his one great passion. Obviously he hadn't found it yet.

Edwin glanced up at me as I entered the office. "Heard you've been working in a strip club," he said with a huge smile on his face.

"Yes I have," I said. "If you want to have a laugh about it, do it now so we never have to revisit this moment again."

"Oh no," said Edwin. "This information is gold. The fact that I've also heard that you've been learning pole dancing is something that I am going to cherish forever, to be brought out at the most inappropriate moments, maybe when your mother is visiting."

I looked at him sourly. "You know, I used to like you. Once upon a time you were nice. Marriage has made you hard and bitter. It changed you, and not for the better."

"But it's fun," said Edwin with that insane smile of happiness on his face. I was joking of course. Edwin and Crystal belonged together and despite the slight bumps in the road, they were both deliriously happy. It was good to see.

"Any chance of me seeing Monique for a moment?" I asked.

"I could organize it for a private demonstration of you pole dancing for just Crystal and me," Edwin said.

"Do you realize how inappropriate that request sounded?" I asked. "Just think on it a moment."

Edwin cocked his head. "I know, but seriously, I've seen you dance and if you bring that lack of coordination to a stripper pole, it would be the funniest entertainment that we would ever see."

"Not going to happen," I said. "Just let Monique know I'm here before I'm forced to go to your wife about your secret fantasy involving me and a stripper pole."

"Spoilsport," said Edwin mildly as he buzzed me through.

Monique was just finishing a phone call when I walked into her office. She waved me into a chair and went back to tapping on the desk with her elegant, manicured fingernails. I always said that Monique was the person I wanted to be when I grew up. She was beautiful, intelligent and had the sharpest business mind of anyone I knew. Most importantly for me at the moment, she also knew everything about everybody who was anybody in LA. I was hoping that meant that she knew about Angela and what she could possibly want with her son.

"So what can I do for you, ma petite?" she asked with that understanding smile that she always used to good effect.

"Do you know of an Angela Copeland?" I asked.

"Copeland," Monique repeated as she tapped her finger against her chin. "The name sounds familiar but I would need to look through some of my records. Any reason you want to know about her?"

"She's Griffin's mother," I said.

"The one who left when he was a baby?" Monique questioned.

I nodded. "For some reason she has turned up out of the blue and wants to connect with her son."

"Maybe that's all it is," said Monique.

I shook my head. "I just sat through the torturous lunch from hell where all she talked about was her life, not one question to Griffin about what has happened in the thirty years since she walked out on him and his father. It was strange. I just got the feeling that she had to connect with him but she didn't care about him. Maybe I'm being a bit cynical but there is something going on here and I don't want to be caught out when it all starts falling apart."

Monique looked at me thoughtfully. "So things are better with you and your young man?" she queried.

"We haven't quite worked things out," I said. "The situation with the mom kind of takes precedence over everything else."

Monique smiled. "It usually does." Suddenly she was all business again. "How is the situation with Alistair going?"

I grimaced. "Same as usual I guess. He's managing to alienate everybody around him. Honestly, if I had to place money on somebody being killed on this job, it would have been him. I do know that he is taking advantage of at least one of the girls."

"Advantage, how?" Monique asked.

"The same advantage those kinds of men always take. He's holding the possibility of a dream just out of sight until he gets what he wants and then he tosses her aside when he has no need for her anymore."

Monique frowned. When she came to Hollywood she had been a stunningly beautiful, innocent young girl and she knew well how someone that naive could be chewed up and spat out by the system.

"Keep an eye on him," she said. "If someone is out there killing lousy human beings, he probably features at the top of the list." She suddenly changed subject. "The bar owner's death, is there any reason to believe that you could be in any danger?"

I scoffed at the thought. There was a world of difference between Hammy and me.

"The only way that I am in any danger is if I walk in on

someone else being murdered," I said. "I don't think I've annoyed anyone enough to get caught in the firing line."

Chapter Twelve

You know there are times when you make sweeping statements and the universe decides that you really need to be shown that you are, in no way, in charge of your fate. I really should have known better than to assure Monique that I was perfectly safe working at a strip club where somebody had already been murdered, especially with my special talent of walking into the wrong place at precisely the wrong time. That thought fleetingly went through my mind when only an hour later I walked into the club to find Denise being held up by a masked gunman. As I walked into the room I was so stunned that I didn't notice the gun being raised. I did however notice the agony as the side of the gun connected with my face. The only thing I saw was the shock in the gunman's eyes. I felt pain ballooning across my cheek and then all I saw as blackness.

I heard my name being called and I willed my eyelids to open, blinking against the harsh light.

"Take it easy, you took quite a knock to the head."

I blinked again and groaned. "Why are you the one I always see when I've been knocked out?"

Dominic gave me that confident grin of his. "Most women are quite happy to wake up and find me watching over them."

I'm sure they did. Dominic was that intriguing mix of rich, powerful, handsome and dangerous. Some women flocked to it. I bolted in the opposite direction. My mother raised me with a very healthy sense of self preservation.

"I'm not most women," I said as I tried to push myself up."

"That's what I find so fascinating about you," Dominic said.

Just what I needed. I sat up and waited for the room to stop spinning.

"What happened?" I lifted my hand to my head to find the massive lump that I was sure had to be there.

"From what we can tell, it looks like you walked in on a robbery," said Dominic.

"What could they possibly be trying to steal?" I asked. "It's a strip club, not a bank. Unless you're looking for a lifetime supply of glitter, there isn't much of a marketable commodity here."

Dominic shrugged. "I have my people looking into it. Don't worry, considering all the cameras in this building, I am sure that the perpetrator will be captured forthwith."

"What are your people going to do with whoever did this?" I asked suspiciously.

Dominic looked hurt by my tone and the accusatory note behind it. I don't know why. I had never professed to having the greatest faith in him.

Denise almost shoved Dominic out of the way.

"Are you hurt badly? Should I get an ambulance? Do you need ice?" she fluttered.

I smiled weakly. "Ice would be good," I said.

Once the two of them had me situated in a chair with a bag of ice against my face, I turned to Denise.

"What happened?" I asked. "I walked in and found some guy holding a gun on you."

Tears shone in Denise's eyes. "I was going through some papers in the office when that person came in waving a gun around. He wouldn't tell me what he wanted. He was becoming very agitated. When you walked in he hit you with the gun. I don't know what he was going to do next. We were so lucky that Mr Caldwell came to see me. He probably saved our lives."

Dominic smiled beatifically at me.

Yeah, I was just lucky.

"I've called the police," said Denise. "They should be here soon."

As if on cue, Griffin and Ramos walked in. Griffin took in the scene with me having an icepack on my face and Dominic acting solicitously towards me. Yet again I could see his jaw tightening. I did not seem to be able to catch a break. I had hoped that with the lunch with his mother, we would be able to get past our issues. Once again Dominic Caldwell was ruining my life, and from the look of the smile on his face, he knew it.

Despite his obvious annoyance, Griffin came over to me, glared at Dominic and then when Dominic grudgingly moved, he squatted down beside me and looked up at my face.

"Are you okay?" he asked gently.

I nodded, hoping that I didn't pick that moment to start crying. Griffin obviously picked up on my distress, because he put an arm around me and gave me a kiss on my non-bruised cheek.

"What am I going to do with you?" he asked.

I shook my head. Apparently speaking was beyond me at the moment. I was blaming it on shock.

At that point Dominic cleared his throat after checking his cell. "Unfortunately it seems that my colleague has been unable to track down the perpetrator."

I could feel my eyes narrowing and the waves of disbelief emanating from Griffin and Ramos were almost palpable. Griffin let go of me and straightened up.

"You're trying to get us to believe that your man lost him."

Dominic gave us a regretful look. "Unfortunately my colleague was unable to keep up with him. We will be discussing this failure."

I could tell that conversation was not going to be pleasant. Another reason, if I actually needed one, never to work for Dominic Caldwell.

Griffin looked down at me, and I could tell that he was torn as to what he should do next.

"I'm not going to hospital," I said.

Griffin sighed in that way he had, that made me feel like he was perfectly well aware that my goal in life was to make his life difficult.

"She was unconscious for a little while," Dominic interjected unhelpfully.

I glared at him balefully and he just smiled innocently back at me.

"You're going to hospital," said Griffin, grabbing my elbow and pulling me up.

Sitting on a hospital bed, I watched Griffin pacing around the room.

"Sit down and try to be patient. You wanted to bring me here. I was quite happy to stay at work and make do with the ice pack," I said, perhaps a little unwisely.

"Yes, as usual that would have been a brilliant plan, and if you have concussion, which of the other staff members have the appropriate first aid qualifications to keep you safe until the paramedics showed up?"

Ah, we had reached the sarcasm point of the proceedings. A smart woman would at this point know to keep her mouth shut. Once again I chose the not so smart move.

"You'd be surprised at the background of some of those women. This economy has been brutal. Sometimes you do what you have to do to support yourself," I said.

Griffin froze. "Is that why you took this job, because of the money? Do you need money?"

I dropped my head. I really had trouble understanding the leaps a man's mind made at times. "Of course I took the job because of the money. Most people do work for the money. There are not many people who are lucky enough to have a job which they love every minute of every day. I'm sure your job has some moments when you wonder what you are doing there and why you have to deal with such difficult people." I took a breath and hoped I didn't feature too often in those moments. "I enjoy the challenge of what I do. I get paid well for what I do. And no, I am not going to take up stripping to supplement my income."

Griffin dropped into a chair. "I really don't like your job," he said heavily.

"Why?" I asked, honestly perplexed.

Griffin looked at me as if he couldn't believe what he was hearing.

"How many times have I ended up sitting in a hospital while you are getting checked out?" he asked. "I'm a cop and I don't get in nearly the same messes that you seem to find yourself in."

"In my defense," I said, "you're a homicide cop. Generally the action has already happened by the time you turn up on the scene."

Griffin's features tightened. When I realized what I'd said I wanted to bang my head against a wall. Once again, open mouth, insert foot.

"I didn't mean that the way it sounded," I said. "I'm just having a bad run at the moment. It's not like it happens all the time. I have clients where everyone around them stays disgustingly healthy throughout the entire assignment. I mean seriously, if I could wish harm on someone it would have been that pop star brat Kai Roth that I worked with six months ago. If anyone was skating on the edge it was him."

Griffin gave a wry smile. "What am I going to do with you?" he asked.

"Not being so angry about the choices I make might be a start," I said. "I don't do these things to deliberately upset you, but I can't keep walking on eggshells around you, thinking you're going to lose it every time I get an assignment you don't like. This is my career. I don't make stupid choices."

Griffin nodded and looked like he was going to say something, but at that moment a doctor walked into the room.

"Well, young lady, your scans look clear but it may be a

good idea for you to have someone close by to keep you company for the rest of the day."

I nodded.

The doctor looked at me critically. "You may also want to rest at home because your face is going to hurt badly for a couple of days."

I was already painfully aware of how much my face was going to hurt.

"She'll stay at home," Griffin growled, glaring at me meaningfully.

I don't know why he was looking at me like that. I wasn't going to argue with him. I very dutifully allowed Griffin to take me home. I didn't even argue when he got called away to work and he organized for a teenage boy to babysit me. Although, after a few minutes of uncomfortable silence as Sean and I looked at each other, I was beginning to realize that maybe I should have argued with him.

"Does it hurt?" asked Sean.

Not the most original of questions, but when the silence gets this uncomfortable you grab onto it with both hands.

"As bad as it looks," I said cautiously.

Silence again and believe me it was beginning to be excruciating. I kept casting through my mind looking for something, anything, to talk about. As usual in these circumstances, I was coming up blank.

Sean looked down at a point on the ground at my feet. I was kind of curious as to what he found so fascinating down there.

"I'm sorry I blamed you for the argument with Griffin," he mumbled.

It took me a while to understand what he was telling me.

"Okay," I said. What else was there to say? If there was one thing I had learned from my time with Sean, it was that he did not take criticism well. After having his mother toss him out of home on the instigation of her deadbeat boyfriend, Sean had a tendency to see any criticism as a prelude to a change of address. He hadn't quite worked out that the residents of the apartment building were not going to let him walk out, at least not until he was educated and we were ready to let our little chick fly. In the case of the building owner, Miss Betsy, I couldn't see that happening soon, maybe not ever. Sean had become a surrogate son to her and I knew the woman packed a big gun and a disturbing attitude when it came to protecting those people that she cared about.

Thankfully, my cell chose that moment to ring and not for the first time I thanked technology's ability to disrupt sometimes awkward moments.

"Where are you?" barked Alistair.

Oops, with all the excitement I forgot that I should have possibly let my boss know that I had finished work for the day.

"I was attacked at the club and have just got home from the hospital," I told him with more patience than he deserved.

There was silence as he accepted that statement and for a fleeting moment I thought that a small amount of empathy may emerge, that somewhere in that blustery bag of ego there was a man of compassion, maybe somewhere deep down.

"I don't care what happened on your time. The club is open and your job requires you to be here," Alistair snarled, obviously impatient with his recalcitrant assistant.

Not for the first time I wondered what it would be like to work with someone that actually possessed some small amount of human kindness and understanding. Of course if I wanted to deal with a client with some consideration for their fellow man, I should have chosen a different town to work in. For a moment I contemplated telling Alistair exactly what he could do with his demand. Monique had a list of clients who, despite my slightly disturbing ability to stumble over dead bodies, would be thrilled to have me on the job. I had no problem at all with leaving Alistair floundering. However, I was currently faced with an evening being babysat by a teenage boy who was having trouble looking me in the eye, and carried the air of someone who wanted to be anywhere but here. I was feeling fine, not even a headache and I didn't really think that the extra care was warranted. The more I thought about it, the more a night at the strip club looked like a better option.

"Due to a blow to the head I am unable to drive," I told Alistair. "If you are able to organize a ride for me to the club, I will be able to attend to assist you." I gave him the address to my apartment and then, leaving him spluttering at my audacity, I turned off my phone, faced Sean and smiled.

"Good news, looks like you've been let off babysitting duty. I'm going into work."

Sean looked perplexed. "Detective Griffin said that I was to stay with you until he could get back here," he said slowly.

"I feel fine," I said. "Don't worry. Griffin won't have a problem at all with this." I smiled brightly, hoping to impart my confidence that Griffin would be totally on board with this plan.

Sean looked skeptical. I know that I think of him as young, but the boy was very perceptive when he wanted to be. That and he knew Griffin.

I sighed dramatically. "Would it make you feel better if I called Griffin and got him to discharge you from your onerous duty for the night?"

Sean rolled his eyes but he nodded.

I had been hoping that he'd tell me that it wasn't necessary to contact Griffin, but I should have known better.

"What's wrong now, Trudie?" Griffin answered his phone impatiently.

Not for the first time I wished I could find an app that could somehow replicate the utter disdain of an old fashioned slammed down telephone. All thoughts of handling this diplomatically went out the window.

"I'm going to work at the club," I said shortly.

There was silence as Griffin obviously digested that piece of information. "Excuse me."

"I'm pretty sure you heard me," I said.

"Okay," he said. "We'll try another tack. Are you nuts? Only this afternoon you were attacked at the club by an unknown assailant who is still at large. You possibly have a concussion and you want to walk straight back into that place, and that isn't even mentioning that there is still a murderer on the loose."

"The attacker wasn't there for me. I was in the wrong place at the wrong time. As for a concussion, I don't even have a headache and just in case I am totally wrong I will be surrounded by people, at least one of them would call a paramedic. As to the murderer, I have nothing to do with Hammy. Whoever killed him is not very likely to come after me. If I really thought that I would be in any danger I would not be going. I'll be fine. I need you to trust me," I said, hoping that for a change he was actually listening to what I had to say.

The silence on the phone was beginning to become slightly painful, when Griffin let out the breath he had obviously been holding while I was putting forward my case.

"When should I pick you up?" he asked and I smiled. He was trying and you know something, that meant a lot.

"Whenever you finish work would be great," I said quietly. "Thank you."

He grunted and I took that to mean that we were going to be okay.

Chapter Thirteen

After assuring Sean that I did not require him to accompany me to work, I set about trying to fix, or at least minimize, the obvious damage to my face. Seeing Hugh's expression when I opened the door did not fill me with confidence that I had managed to hide the bruising.

"Does it really look that bad?" I asked.

Hugh ducked his head and I had to give the man credit. I could see the cogs in his brain working as he tried to decide on a diplomatic answer.

I decided to let him off the hook. "Don't bother answering, I looked in a mirror before opening the door." The bruise itself was no longer so obvious. It was the heavily caked on makeup that now drew attention to the area. Short of hiding out in my apartment, there didn't seem to be much that I could do about it. I had tried to make it look natural, but there is a point where you need to admit that you are fighting a losing battle and I had reached that point about ten minutes earlier.

"Does it hurt?" asked Hugh as we got in his car.

"A little," I said. "I cannot believe that I walked into that. I didn't even have a chance to duck."

"Do they know what the guy wanted?" asked Hugh.

I shook my head. "I must have walked in at the start because Denise said he hadn't had a chance to say anything yet."

"Why didn't you tell Alistair to shove it when he called? If I looked like that there is no way that I'd be going out in public," Hugh said as he maneuvered the car through the LA traffic.

I would have been a lot more offended at that statement if I wasn't painfully aware of just how bad I looked at the moment.

I shrugged my shoulders. I knew my time with Alistair was limited and knowing there was an expiration date made it easier to accede to some of his more irrational demands. That was the beauty of my job. I knew that no matter how lousy an assignment was, it wasn't going to last forever.

Considering the change in management, Hammys was still exactly the same as it had been for the last several weeks. Same dancers, same acts, same regular clients, and there was Travis standing in a corner, his eyes sweeping the club. When they alighted on me a combination of amusement and frustration crossed over his face. After checking in with Alistair and discovering that he didn't have any actual work for me to do, that he just wanted me there in case he needed me, I went to find Travis.

"You know, the amount of time you spend here is seriously staring to disturb me," I said as I came up beside him.

His eyes crinkled but I could see his concern as he focused on the bruise on my cheek.

I sighed. "How did you know?" I asked.

Travis shrugged. "People tell me things."

"And you came here tonight because?"

Travis grinned. "I know you, Trudie, and I know the nutcase you are working for. There is no way that he was going to let you have the night off and I don't think he's quite annoyed you enough to tell him where to shove his job."

"I think you'd be surprised," I murmured.

"Getting to the end of that almost limitless amount of patience that you seem to have?" asked Travis.

I nodded. "I don't even know why we are here. I get that Alistair thinks this is going to be a gritty expose on a part of life that most people want to ignore, but the longer we are here the more exploitative it seems to be. He's playing with people's lives here. Sooner or later someone is going to bite back."

"You think that is what happened to Hammy?" Travis asked speculatively.

I had to laugh at the gleam in his eye. Travis was one of, if not the best private investigator in LA. He was the go to guy for divorce cases and he was good at his job. Despite that, he was a cop through to the bone. If it hadn't been for some situation between him and Griffin, most of which hadn't been fully explained to me, he would have still been a cop, puzzling over these sort of cases.

"I think that considering the way that Hammy treated the women here, it is a miracle that someone didn't kill him a very long time ago. From what I understand, Hammy has owned this place for decades, more than enough time for there to be a list of people who wanted to see him dead," I said.

"Sure, but strangulation with a whip kind of sounds a bit personal to me," murmured Travis.

I shrugged. Hammy had dealt badly with people overall. He exploited and belittled the women who worked here and he ripped off the clientele. The fact that he had allowed Alistair to film here at all gave an indication of how little regard he had for anyone who walked into this club. The only surprising thing about Hammy's death was that it hadn't happened years before now.

"What the hell is he doing here?" I could see Travis's eyes widen as he looked over at one of the booths.

I had to stop myself from dropping my head in frustration. Dominic Caldwell and one of his colleagues had taken a seat in a booth which gave a wide view of the entire bar.

"I don't believe it," I muttered. Everywhere I turned these days that man seemed to be popping into my life.

Travis turned to me speculatively. "Please tell me that you don't know Dominic Caldwell."

I really wished I could tell him that. Knowing Dominic Caldwell was one of those things that I could have lived my whole life without accomplishing and been happy with.

"I've had the pleasure of meeting him," I muttered.

Actually it was less of a pleasure and more of a terrifyingly traumatic experience which involved me being kidnapped and helping him find a priceless heirloom that had been stolen by an ex-girlfriend. That chance kidnapping seemed to have spawned, in Dominic's mind anyway, some kind of weird relationship.

"I think I'd better find out what he's doing here," I said as I started to walk away.

Travis grabbed my arm. "Are you nuts?" he said forcefully. "Do you have any idea who that man is?"

"Rich, bad guy who doesn't seem to believe the laws of this country apply to him. On the radar of most of the law enforcement agencies in this country. The second he sits down and speaks to me, Griffin gets a heads up and I get in trouble. Does that pretty much cover it?"

Travis was giving me that look of his again. The one where he can't believe that one person is able to get themselves into such messed up situations. As I started to walk towards Dominic, he started to follow me. I turned around and put my hand onto the middle of his chest to stop him.

"No," I said.

"What?" he replied, looking at me innocently.

"I don't have any choice dealing with Dominic. He knows me and I can pretty much guarantee that even if I didn't go and talk to him, in a very short period of time, that colleague of his would be coming over here to invite me to join him. You, on the other hand, can stand here and stay blissfully under his radar. Believe me, if I had a choice I would much rather be you than me."

Travis glared at me incredulously. "You cannot think for a moment that I am going to let you just walk up to Dominic Caldwell and sit down with him."

There it was again. I loved how the men in my life kept tossing out that word 'let' as if they actually had any say at all.

"You are going to stay here and watch over the proceedings with that glare that you obviously enjoy throwing around. I can handle Dominic, but if you come over with me you will just make the situation unnecessarily difficult."

Travis stared at me and, for a moment, I was worried that he really wasn't going to listen to me and would start something with Dominic. If I thought Griffin was annoyed with me now, that would be nothing if a brawl started in a strip club between Travis and Dominic because of me. I really didn't need that kind of grief.

I could see the moment that Travis relented. "I am not taking my eyes off you for a moment," he growled. "You are not to go anywhere with the man at all. That is the only way that you are going to get me to stay here and not come over there with you."

I let out the breath that I was holding. I liked that plan, I loved that plan. There is no way that I would willingly go anywhere with Dominic Caldwell. However, the man had kidnapped me twice, so I knew he was not above trying to drag me out of here if he thought he needed to. Having Travis watching proceedings and ensuring that didn't happen gave me a little bit of confidence as I walked up to Dominic's booth, which I usually didn't have when dealing with him.

"Good evening, Trudie. You're looking lovely tonight," Dominic boomed as I came up to him.

This was just one of the myriad of reasons why I didn't trust this man. He was able to make that statement without one ounce of sarcasm. Looking over at his colleague, I could see the disbelief on his face. I knew perfectly well what I looked like. I had so much makeup caked over one side of my face that I was going to need a trowel to take it off. Anyone with two functioning eyes would be able to see the lie in Dominic's statement, but he gave every indication that he completely believed what he just said.

No wonder the man was so rich. He could sell anything to anybody.

"Why are you here?" I asked, knowing that the chances of me getting an honest answer were very slim, but feeling the need to ask anyway.

"I had business dealings with Mr Pollard. We were close to finalizing a deal on this land. I am hoping to continue those discussions with the bereaved widow. Please join me."

Dominic waved his hand to where his colleague was sitting. I raised an eyebrow and almost laughed at the put out expression on the man's face. I didn't feel any sympathy for anyone Dominic described as one of his colleagues. I didn't have the best history with Dominic's colleagues, who most law-abiding people had other terms for. I had terms for them too, most of my terms couldn't be used in polite company though. I took the vacated seat and settled in for Dominic's own brand of fiction.

"So, did you want to explain why you are really here?" I asked Dominic, keeping an eye on his colleague and the fact Travis was watching the exchange with an avid amount of interest.

Dominic sighed and that sigh more than anything else encouraged me to believe that I may be getting, if not an honest answer, at least one which had a few shards of truth in it. "Despite the fact that your ability to consistently end up in the wrong place at the wrong time is highly entertaining, today's episode has given me some cause for concern. I am looking into my interests here anyway so I just felt that it would behoove me to keep an eye on you as well."

Lucky me. There were moments in my life when I felt an overwhelming urge to run and hide. Lately, most of those moments had involved this man and today was no different. Dominic put out a hand to push back my hair which had fallen forward and was covering my cheek.

"I am very unhappy that this happened to you," he said

and I could hear the ominous tone threaded through that statement.

I really hoped that Griffin found whoever did this first because I didn't think my assailant would enjoy whatever was being promised in Dominic's eyes. I pulled back from the man, not for the first time cursing the way he had ended up in my life. Travis had started moving towards us, obviously unhappy with the fact that Dominic had got a bit too close for his liking. I stood up quickly.

"Don't do anything that's going to get you arrested," I warned.

Dominic burst out laughing and even flustered as I was I could see the irony in that statement.

"Thank you," he said smiling. "There are not many people in this world who would make that statement to me without it being a joke."

I quickly walked away, intercepting Travis and putting my hand on his chest to stop his approach.

"Please don't get involved," I said.

Travis looked down at me. "Someday you are really going to need to tell me why you are on touching and laughing terms with Dominic Caldwell. You do realize that all of that comes under risky behavior."

"Believe me when I say that none of it is invited."

"Then that is worse," said Travis. "I don't think that you understand exactly who that man is."

"Believe me I do," I said. I was very much aware of the kind of man that Dominic was. Unfortunately I didn't seem to be able to shake him. The door to the club opened and I dropped my head.

"Excuse me," I said and headed to the bar.

"Crystal," I said patiently. "Why have you dragged your husband into a strip club?"

"Well." Crystal was giving herself whiplash as her head twisted, trying to take in all the sights around her. "You've been telling me about your work here and it sounded so exciting that I thought it would be great to see what you've been doing.

"Kind of like bring your crazy friend to work day," I said.

"But better," Crystal said. "Do they serve food here?"

I shuddered. "I really would not suggest ordering food here," I said. "See the hand sanitizing lotion that seems to be dotted all around the bar. There's a reason there is so much of it around the place. If you're hungry, go home and have something to eat. There's less chance of you ending up getting your stomach pumped."

Crystal smiled, that irrepressible look on her face showed me that she was determined that nothing was going to interfere with her need to take care of me. I gave up and turned to Edwin.

"I am so sorry you got dragged here."

Edwin shrugged. "There are worse things I could be doing tonight."

I wasn't so sure.

Crystal pulled my hair back and looked critically at my cheek. "I hope Griffin is going to do something about this."

I pulled my hair back and let it fall forward, covering as much of my cheek as I possibly could. "How did you know?"

"Sean," said Edwin sympathetically.

Of course. I hadn't even thought to try to stifle Sean's willingness to share news with just about everyone. In fact, I was kind of surprised that Miss Betsy wasn't here.

"Miss Betsy would have been here, but she had a meeting with some of the members of her gardening club tonight," Crystal said as if reading my mind.

I had to admit, I was kind of relieved. Miss Betsy was my landlady but in a previous life had been a stuntwoman during Hollywood's less than stellar workplace safety era. Lovely woman, but you never knew how she would react to anything.

"Please tell me Sean hasn't told anyone else," I

moaned.

Edwin pointed behind me. "I have a feeling your boss knows."

I froze. Not Monique. Of course, she knew where I was working but I don't think I could handle the sight of my boss, Monique Petit, the epitome of classical style and grace, standing in the middle of Hammy's Gentleman's Club. I turned around and let out the breath that I had been holding. Oh thank goodness. It was Jorge. Jorge was one of the security people who work for Monique. He and I were regularly found working with each other. According to Jorge that's because, thanks to my habit of finding dead bodies, the other security guys on staff were a little frightened to work with me. Just in case I have some weird voodoo killing power that nobody has picked up on yet. Of course, according to him, he is just so brave that he is willing to face death with me at any time.

I frowned as I noticed the woman sitting with him.

"Excuse me," I said to Crystal and Edwin as I walked over to Jorge at the table he was sitting at.

"What are you doing here, Jorge?" I asked, although I had a pretty good idea.

"I just thought I'd have a look at the show," Jorge said, trying desperately not to look at me directly.

"With your wife," I said as I looked over at the woman sitting next to him.

"How did you know she was my wife?" he asked curiously.

"Because I know you, Jorge, and I know how devoted you are to her. No way would you be coming to a strip club with some random woman."

The woman laughed and held out a hand. "I'm Linda" she said.

I took it and shook it firmly. "Hi, Linda, I'm Trudie. I work with your husband and I'm guessing I'm the reason you got dragged here tonight. I am so sorry." I seemed to be apologizing to everyone this evening.

I turned to Jorge. "Your wife is home from being deployed overseas. Why did you take a job tonight?"

Jorge looked confused.

"I know Monique would have told you not to say anything but let me take a guess. My little run in with whoever hit me has got Monique concerned for my safety. I have no idea how she found out about it but that's Monique, she knows everything. She contacted you and asked you to work here tonight and keep an eye on me. How am I going so far?"

"Pretty much totally right," Jorge mumbled. "Linda wasn't supposed to come in until tomorrow, so I figured there was no problem with me working tonight."

"But I got in early to surprise him." Linda took up the story. "He was going to cancel but he's been keeping me entertained with stories about what you've been doing, so I thought this was the perfect chance for me to see the great Trudie Eyre in action."

I turned to Jorge. "What exactly have you been telling your wife about me?" I asked.

"Nothing that wasn't completely true," said Jorge.

"Strangely enough, that doesn't comfort me," I said. "You know I'll be fine if you want to get going."

Both Jorge and Linda shook their heads, their eyes trained on the bruise on my cheek.

I tried again. "I'd rather you two spent tonight anywhere but at a strip club."

Linda laughed. "I'm an MP with the US Marine Corps. Believe me, I've seen the inside of my share of strip clubs. I'm not going to be shocked by anything I see in here."

I was shocked on a regular basis and I had been in this building solidly for the last two weeks. I took that fact as a good thing.

I looked up and groaned.

"What's wrong?" asked Jorge, as both he and Linda went on alert.

"Nothing that I can't deal with," I said. "Please excuse

me."

I walked over to the entrance of the club where Griffin's father was standing, looking far more uncomfortable than I expected an ex-cop to look.

"Do I even need to ask, Lee?"

"I can't believe you thought for one moment that my boy was going to be okay with this," Lee said, pinning me with his gaze.

"I didn't, that would be why we are arguing at the moment," I said.

Lee softened. "I know, thank you for going with Jake to see his mother."

I nodded. Really what could I say? He had fallen in love with the woman and married her once. Regardless of how it turned out, she was the mother of his child.

Lee's eyes trained on the bruising on my cheek.

"Don't," I said.

"Don't what?" I could tell Lee was holding on to his temper by a thread.

"Don't get angry when there is nothing that can be done about it. Griffin will be looking into it and I'm depending on him to do the right thing," I said.

Lee didn't answer. My experience with the Griffin men meant that I knew this was not a good thing. Before I could argue the point some more, I could see Alistair had finally worked out a reason that he had dragged me in here. He was standing at the door that led to the dressing rooms, angrily gesturing in my general direction. Of course, most of the things that Alistair did were done angrily.

"Look," I said. "I've got to get back to work."

Lee nodded, his eyes swinging back and forth intently. I could see that he had reverted to cop mode and it was interesting on occasions like this to see exactly how much like his son he was.

Chapter Fourteen

Finding that Alistair had managed to upset another of the girls did not come as a complete shock. What was new, however, was finding that Denise was about ready to tear him apart. In the last two weeks, Hammy hadn't cared one bit what Alistair had done with the girls as long as they were able to get on stage and earn him some money. Thankfully, Denise seemed to be made of sterner stuff and she was determined to protect the girls from Alistair.

"What's wrong?" I asked Hugh who was watching the proceedings with unabashed delight.

"Well, Alistair was talking to Brandi about the reason why she was stripping. She started talking about her dreams to be a dancer. He interrupted and started on about some affair that she was having with Hammy, how she had sold her soul, and then it all went downhill from there."

I nodded, understanding how this was exactly like all the interviews that Alistair had done over the last two weeks. I did not understand why he was considered such a popular documentary maker. The man had a gift with getting everybody offside. I could see how people would forgive that aggressiveness when he was targeting the government or big corporations, like he had done in all his films up until now. But that hard hitting style did not work when you were dealing with people who were just struggling to make ends meet any way they could. At best he came off as insensitive. At worst it exposed exactly the type of person he was, self-interested and judgmental. I had spent two weeks trying to deal with the fallout of these interviews. Not for the first time I wondered what I was doing here. He didn't need a personal assistant. He needed a social worker, an etiquette coach and some major therapy.

Hugh watched me keenly. "You knew about Brandi and Hammy didn't you?"

I looked at him but didn't confirm. Regardless of what I personally thought of the older Hammy sleeping with Brandi, who must be just barely into her twenties, it was their business, not mine. Anyway, I'd only just found out after the fact, thank goodness. Considering my talent of walking in on people at awkward moments, I was grateful that I had missed that particular scene.

"I need coffee," Alistair barked at me.

It was good to know that the reason he had insisted on me being here was because of the vital work I was accomplishing. I went to the dressing room where the coffee machine was. It was pretty much the only benefit that the girls working here had got from Alistair upending their lives. In the first week I had managed to get him to spring for a coffee machine. Of course, the reasoning I had used was that it would be so much better if I made it myself with a machine on site, rather than having to go to the nearest coffee shop. This message was brought home to him after a truly awful cup of coffee that I had got for him from a store nearby. Admittedly, I had bought it and left it for half an hour before giving it to him. That may have had something to do with his unusual generosity in this area. Working on the coffee, I could hear sobbing coming from a corner of the seemingly empty dressing room. I followed the noise and found Brandi sitting on the floor in a closet.

"Hey," I said gently. "Is there anything I can do to help?"

I don't know what I said, but my query only managed to send her into a fresh wave of sobbing. I sat down next to her and put an arm around her shoulder.

"It can't be that bad," I said. "Alistair's a jerk. Whatever he said comes from a really damaged part of his soul."

I knew I was being a bit hard on the man I was supposed to be working for, but frankly if he had reduced Brandi to tears, again, then he was the kind of person who kicked puppies for fun.

Brandi looked up at me, smiling through her tears, until her eyes found the bruising on my cheek and then she dissolved into wrenching sobs again.

"I am so sorry," she said between gasps for breath.

"What are you sorry for?" I asked.

"Your face. You shouldn't have got hurt. That isn't right. You've been so nice to us, especially when he is so mean."

I didn't want to tell her that, regrettably, that was my job description. I was the one who picked up the pieces when my clients showed the world how wonderful they were. It was kind of a Hollywood version of good cop, bad cop. Except in our case it was more like good cop, damaged beyond belief cop. Brandi just dissolved into more tears.

"I have a boyfriend," she said.

I wasn't surprised. A lot of the girls did have boyfriends, and Brandi had that pretty sweetness to her that men loved.

"He was the one that told me if I slept with Hammy we could get some money out of him."

Ah, the boyfriend was the special kind of slime that some of the girls attracted.

"Why would he want me to do that?" Brandi said. "He told me if I did it that we could get me out of here and start our life together."

What could I say? The guy was taking advantage of her trust and love. I knew it and deep down Brandi knew it as well. That was probably the reason for the never ending waterworks that she seemed to have.

"Trudie, Alistair's yelling for you. Again." I could tell that Amber had gone past the point of tolerance for Alistair. It was amazing how quickly a relationship could turn into complete and utter contempt.

"Over here," I said.

Amber looked down at the two of us sitting on the floor in a closet and I could physically see her repress the sigh.

"Alistair?" she said.

I nodded and shrugged at the same time. I'm pretty sure Alistair set her off, but there were some deep seated issues here.

Amber squatted down beside us. "Alistair is going nuts out there. Something set him off and he's taking it out on everyone else. Can you go out there and do whatever it is you do before someone kills him."

I grimaced and Amber realized what she had said.

"Sorry, poor choice of words. I'll take care of Brandi."

I nodded, got up, grabbed the coffee and went out to face Alistair.

"Where have you been?" he snarled, grabbing the coffee out of my hands.

"Putting out fires," I said noncommittally.

He shoved the digital voice recorder that he seemed to carry with him everywhere, into my hand. "I need the notes on this transcribed. I also need you to watch some of the show and take notes on your impressions." He obviously saw my confused expression. "I want to get a woman's perspective of how she feels when watching another woman performing on stage."

I had to hide my distaste at the gleam in his eye. I really was not aware of a way that Alistair could make this project any more uncomfortable for all involved.

Grabbing my laptop, I found an empty booth at the back and started working on the transcribing. I also kept an eye on the stage so I could do the notes that Alistair requested. Unfortunately, I kept being distracted by the disjointed effects from the recorder. It was one of those sound activated ones so there were always problems with the flow of conversation. It also had a tendency to activate at random noises.

Taking a quick break, I looked up and had to smile. As I looked around the room I spotted Travis in a corner, watching everyone with that studied look he had. Dominic Caldwell had taken up position in one of the booths with one of his colleagues keeping him company and keeping the women away from him. Jorge was sitting with his wife and both of them were watching me as if expecting to have to spring into action at any point. Crystal and Edwin were getting a drink. Edwin had the long suffering look on his face of a man who got dragged to a strip club by his wife and he had no idea how to deal with the situation. His eyes kept darting around as he tried manfully to avoid looking at the naked women while his wife was standing next to him. Lee was shadowing me around the club. When I moved, he did. If I didn't know how sweet it was that he was here to protect me, I would definitely find it creepy.

A good proportion of tonight's clientele were attending purely to make sure that I was safe. While it gave me a warm and fuzzy feeling to know so many people cared about me, I really hoped that the girls working weren't depending on tips tonight, because takings were going to be a bit on the lean side.

Chapter Fifteen

I lowered my head and went back to work. To be perfectly honest I was just waiting for this night to be over. My cheek was throbbing and I had the beginnings of a headache.

"You know the makeup doesn't help."

I looked up to find an older woman standing at the table.

"I'm sorry," I said, self-consciously ducking my head and letting my hair fall forward.

The woman's face creased in sympathy. "You've put makeup on to hide the bruise. It looks like it's wiping off. It's very obvious at the moment."

I felt embarrassed. I shouldn't have and I was mad at myself that I was. This woman was a stranger but I still felt that I had to explain.

"I'm not one of the dancers. I'm an assistant. I walked in on a robbery today. Bad timing." I indicated the bruise.

"I'm sorry," the woman said. "I work with a lot of the women in this industry and see a lot of bruises. I have a tendency to walk up to people and talk when I shouldn't."

She had kind eyes and I always thought the world needed more people who cared about strangers. "My name is Trudie," I said.

"Susan," said the woman. "Can I sit down?"

I indicated the seat with my hand and she took it.

"I'm really sorry. I shouldn't have assumed. I work for a church group and we help a lot of women who are abused. Most don't talk about it. I've learned that sometimes I need to initiate the conversation," Susan said.

I shrugged. "I understand. I'm sitting in this place with a massive bruise on my face. It's actually kind of nice that someone cares enough not to look in the other direction.

Believe me I've had a few of those looks today."

Susan smiled but quickly sobered. "How exactly did you get that bruise?"

"Like I said, I came into work and there was some guy holding a gun on the owner. I walked in, not knowing what was going on. He reacted and hit my across the face. Next thing, it was lights out for me," I said.

"This kind of place is not really a safe one to be in," said Susan.

"Do you normally come to places like this looking for women?" I asked.

Susan shook her head. "I used to work here many years ago. I got out because somebody cared enough to help me. I come back here sometimes to offer someone else the same opportunity."

"Do you get taken up on it very often?" I asked, curious and thinking this was the kind of story that Alistair should be concentrating on. No chance I was going to tell him about it though. I'd had enough tears to cope with today and Susan seemed nice. No way did she deserve the Alistair treatment.

Susan shook her head again. "Usually I don't get much of a chance. Hammy chases me out but I heard that he died and there is a new owner so I thought I'd give it a go."

"Hammy's wife, Denise, owns the place now," I said and noted the look of sympathy that crossed Susan's face.

"Do you know Denise?" I asked.

"I knew her when she first married Hammy," Susan said. "We were both dancers back then. It was a long time ago. I remember that she was so in love with Hammy."

"I don't see it," I mused. "Denise does not seem the kind of person to fall for Hammy. I worked with him for a couple of weeks and I didn't understand why any woman would willingly be in his company for longer than five minutes."

Susan chuckled. "He was a charmer wasn't he? He

could turn it on when he wanted to though and he wanted Denise. Do you know about his mother?"

"A little," I said.

"That woman ruled him with an iron fist. She wanted him to get married, he got married. She wanted grandchildren, he got Denise pregnant."

"Denise has a child?" I interrupted.

Susan shrugged her shoulders. "This is the part of the story which proves that Hammy had no redeeming qualities. His mother wanted grandchildren so he got Denise pregnant, but then his mother died. He didn't really want that baby so he gave Denise an ultimatum, him or the child."

"Which did she choose?" I asked, totally enthralled with the story.

Susan shrugged. "I don't know for sure. What I do know though is that she came back to him begging for a second chance and there didn't seem to be a child in the picture."

"But they didn't end up together. I thought that they had broken up years ago."

"A few months after she came back he dumped her," Susan said.

"So she didn't end up with anything," I said softly.

Susan nodded. "She made the wrong choice. A lot of women do when it comes to men, especially in this industry."

I nodded and, remembering Brandi's tears, I made a rash decision. "If you're looking for someone who needs help, I think I have a candidate," I said. "Just wait here."

In the dressing room I found Brandi bravely trying to use makeup to hide the damage from her crying jag. She was having just as much success as I had been with my bruise. I sat down on a chair next to her.

"Brandi, do you want to be here?" I asked.

"I have to," said Brandi. "I need to bring money in. It's the only way for me to get out of this life. If I can just bring in some more."

The tears started rolling down her face again. At this point I didn't know whether I was going to make things better or worse.

"I've met a lady out the front, she used to work here a long time ago and she got out. I think that it might be a good idea for you to talk to her," I said gently.

Brandi shook her head. "I can't" she said. "I'm stuck here."

"No you're not. You just need to start making your own choices. This boyfriend of yours let you be with Hammy for money. What does that tell you about him?"

I had no problem with the dancers if they chose to be here. I did have a problem with them having their choices taken away. Everyone could see that Brandi was desperately unhappy. To put it down in bald economic terms, she had the lowest tips of any of the performers. That was simply because her whole demeanor screamed that she really did not want to be here and the customers could see it. In this job, enthusiasm counted.

Brandi started tearing up again. "Do you really think she can help me?" she whispered.

I tried to use my words carefully. "I think you have a choice here. I'm just letting you know that there is another option sitting out the front."

Brandi wiped her hand across her eyes. "I can't keep doing this," she said and I could hear a thread of steel weaving through her voice. "I want to meet your friend."

When Susan saw Brandi following me back to the booth, I could see the smile playing on her lips.

"Brandi, this is Susan. She used to work here and I think she may be able to help you with your problem," I said.

"Would you like to grab a coffee with me at the diner across the street?" Susan asked gently.

Brandi nodded and Susan stood up. Susan smiled at me as they walked towards the door. Watching them leave, I hoped Brandi found her way.

"Where's Brandi going?" asked Hugh from behind me.

I jumped. "Could you please not do that. You need to make more noise when you walk up behind people. You gave me a scare."

Hugh smiled. Looking around the room I made a hand gesture to indicate to my team of protectors that I was okay. My jumping in fright at Hugh walking up behind me had put them all on edge and they had started moving in my direction. Lucky for me, Hugh didn't notice that he had almost become the victim of a mass attack.

"Where's Brandi going?" Hugh repeated.

"I think she needs a break," I said vaguely. "You know, Alistair." It was easy to blame Alistair for absolutely anything that went wrong. Stripper upset, Alistair's fault. Legalities a bit blurry, Alistair's fault. Zombie apocalypse, Alistair's fault.

"How much longer are you staying tonight?" he asked.

I shrugged. "As long as it takes to finish off this work for Alistair. Why?"

"Just wondering when you wanted to head home," he said.

I smiled. "Thanks, Hugh. My boyfriend is supposed to be picking me up and if he can't, I have a feeling that I have other options." Four other options to be exact. Five if I included Dominic Caldwell. Of course I would have to really be desperate to get in a car with him.

"As long as you're okay," Hugh said and I was touched that he hadn't taken me at my word and bolted the first chance he got.

"All good," I said. "You enjoy the rest of your night."

As he walked off I started back into my work, determined to try to translate some of the nonsensical sounds on Alistair's recorder.

Chapter Sixteen

When Griffin walked in and found my entourage of protectors, I almost laughed at the incredulous look on his face. He stopped near the doorway to speak to Lee who bolted with a pathetically grateful look on his face. Edwin grabbed Crystal's hand, waved in my direction and dragged her out with a similar expression to Lee. Jorge looked in my direction and I nodded, using our nonverbal communication to tell him that the boyfriend of mine that he didn't like was taking over guard duty, so he could leave the strip club and go home with his wife. Travis nodded in my direction and followed Jorge out. Dominic seemed to be in two minds, but he raised a glass in my direction, drank it down and headed out the door. Griffin kept his eyes on Dominic and Travis as he came over and stood in front of me.

"You really know how to clear a room, don't you?" I said.

"What were all those people doing here?" asked Griffin. "I swear the only one I set on you was Dad."

"I know," I said. "Jorge was sent by Monique on assignment, Travis was just here because he always seems to be here and Dominic was continuing in his campaign to freak me out in that special way he has."

"And Edwin and Crystal?" Griffin asked.

I shrugged my shoulders. "I'm assuming they were here protecting me, but knowing the way Crystal embraces new and different experiences, it could have been just another night out for them."

"I sometimes feel sorry for Edwin," Griffin said.

I snorted. "Don't be, he's so in love with Crystal he'd find a way to the moon for her if she asked."

There was an uncomfortable silence. Oh yes, the little

elephant in our relationship. I knew Griffin cared for me very much but I just wasn't entirely sure whether he loved me. My cheek throbbed. I really didn't have the energy to deal with this at the moment.

"Trudie," Griffin said and I steeled myself. I did not like the tone in his voice at all.

"Trudie," came another voice and I almost wept with relief.

I looked up to find Susan and Brandi standing near the booth. Susan had a very worried expression on her face and Brandi seemed terrified. They both looked at Griffin and, if it was possible, Brandi's eyes went wider.

"You're a cop," she said accusingly to Griffin.

Griffin nodded.

"This is Detective Griffin. He's my....friend." I finished off weakly.

Now I had Brandi looking at me as if I was consorting with the enemy, Griffin looked like I'd stabbed him through the heart and Susan just looked confused. I really should write a book on how to alienate people in the fewest number of steps possible.

"I don't know if I can do this," Brandi muttered as she started stepping backwards.

Susan caught her arm. "It is your choice," she said. "You were just saying that you want to do the right thing. This is the start."

Brandi stopped for a moment and looked as if she was gathering her courage.

"I know who hurt you," she said quietly.

I saw Griffin tense and, knowing how scared Brandi must be and how little it would take for her to bolt, I smiled gently at her.

"Do you want to sit down and talk to us about it?" I asked.

Brandi nodded and slid into the booth next to me. Susan took a seat beside her and continued holding the young girl's hand.

"I don't know where to start," said Brandi, her eyes focused on the table in front of her.

"Just start at the beginning and tell them everything that you told me," said Susan soothingly.

Brandi took in a calming breath. "I've been sleeping with Hammy for the last few months. When I first started here he paid me a lot of special attention. I don't know what it was about me, but he was different to me than he was with the other girls. My boyfriend came to the show once and he saw how Hammy was with me. He said if I started seeing Hammy it would help me and maybe we could use it to our advantage. Hammy was sweet. He treated me really nice. Nobody has ever treated me like that so it wasn't really hard for me to get involved with him. We were seeing each other and then one day he said that he was in love with me. He wanted to marry me."

That surprised me considering the man already had a wife who he had treated appallingly badly. Susan caught my eye over the top of Brandi's head. I think we both agreed that Brandi may have had a lucky escape.

"Did you want to marry him?" I asked.

Brandi shook her head. "He was nice to me and everything but I didn't want to marry him."

"Did you tell him that?" I asked.

Brandi nodded. "I told him I wasn't ready to get married."

"How did he react?" I asked.

"He understood," said Brandi. "He said that he knew it was sudden but that he loved me and was willing to wait. He said that to prove how much he loved me he was going to write up a new will and leave everything to me."

That caught Griffin's attention. Changes in wills by murder victims always caught Griffin's attention. "Had he actually changed his will?" barked Griffin. Much as I knew that Ramos did not like me, at least she had a gentle touch to her when interrogating suspects. Griffin was like a bulldog. At least this time I wasn't the one on the receiving end of the interrogation.

Brandi's eyes widened. "He showed it to me the day before he died. He said he was going to get it signed. I don't know what happened to it after that. When his wife showed up with the old will, I just figured that he never got a chance to sign it."

The innocence in her eyes was breathtaking. On the other hand, I could see the various scenarios playing out in Griffin's head. Changing a will definitely brought a whole new side to a murder case.

"My boyfriend didn't believe that nobody could find the new will. He said if we had this place we would be set for life. He could run it and I would be the headline act."

I could see how little Brandi liked that idea.

Brandi's eyes cut to my cheek and I could see tears welling up in her eyes again. "He came here today looking for the new will. He was sure that Denise had hidden it."

Just like that, everything fell into place.

"Your boyfriend was the one who hit Trudie, wasn't he?" said Griffin softly.

I wish I could say that softness was due to him being sensitive enough to realize the precarious emotional condition that Brandi was in. However, I knew the man and I knew that tone marked a wellspring of anger that he was holding inside.

Brandi nodded. Thankfully she wasn't aware of the emotion Griffin was holding in check or else she may have been a little less forthcoming with her information.

"What's your boyfriend's name?" asked Griffin who seemed to have taken over the situation.

"Jayden Johnson, everyone calls him JJ," Brandi said and I could tell it took a lot out of her to do that. "He was just looking for the will and then Denise came in and when Trudie walked in he panicked. I really don't think he meant to hurt her so badly." Brandi pleaded her boyfriend's case.

I could tell that there was still a part of Brandi that was unwilling to let the relationship with Jayden go, regardless of how dysfunctional it looked to those of us on the outside. Susan put an arm around Brandi's shoulders as Griffin got up and started barking orders into his cell. I assumed he was talking to Ramos. I wondered if she put up with his tone as well as I did.

Susan was comforting Brandi as Griffin came back.

"Brandi, is there somewhere you can go tonight?" asked Griffin, finally working out that a little bit of gentleness was the way to deal with this witness.

"She can stay with me," said Susan.

Brandi smiled at her appreciatively. I hoped that Brandi was going to take the opportunity that Susan was offering.

Griffin turned to me. "I need to take you home now, Trudie."

"Just give me a second," I said and quickly downloaded the rest of the audio files from Alistair's recorder.

After returning the recorder to Alistair, I informed him that I was going to go home and would most likely be working from there tomorrow, as my face had gone past painful and was now in the excruciating point of the healing process. Alistair wasn't happy with my proclamation but as I had never actually seen Alistair happy with anything, I wasn't even going to bother trying.

Griffin drove me home with single minded determination. He might have been in the car with me, but I knew that at this moment his mind was with Ramos as they were looking at a break in the case. At least it kept him from returning to whatever it was that he had been about to say to me before Brandi interrupted us at the club. I wasn't going to take it personally.

Chapter Seventeen

What I did take personally was him saying goodbye and driving off with barely a word to me when we got to the apartment building. I had come to an understanding about how important Griffin's work was to him. Right at this moment, I was sore and now that I thought about it, I was hungry. I hadn't had anything to eat since that painful lunch with Griffin's mother which seemed to have happened a long time ago. Walking into my apartment, I threw my keys and laptop on the table and headed straight for the freezer. Pulling out the tub of ice cream, I figured it could perform double duty. I could eat the ice cream to satisfy my hunger and I could hold the tub against my cheek to try to calm down the bruising. The ice cream would be multitasking. Definitely a good plan.

Sitting on the floor eating ice cream out of the tub while holding the tub against my face, I contemplated exactly how this assignment had ended up with me in such a ludicrous position.

My cell rang, interrupting my contemplation. I was caught. One of my hands was holding a spoonful of ice cream heading for my mouth. The other one was holding the tub pressed against my face and was giving me sweet, sweet relief. I had to make a choice. With a sigh I put the tub down and put the spoon in my mouth as I grabbed for the phone.

"Ma petite, you are finally home."

I swallowed the ice cream. "How do you know that, Monique?" You'd think after all the time that I had known Monique that I would have finally worked out how she seems to know everything. "You have surveillance in my house, don't you?" I said, the horror in my voice evident. I really hoped she didn't. Sitting on the floor in my living room with a tub of ice cream held against my face, while scooping spoonfuls out to eat was definitely not one of my finest moments, and I really hoped nobody ever saw me like this.

Monique laughed. "Of course I don't, ma petite. Jorge gave me a report and I gave you enough time to get home. Simple really."

Of course. Simple.

"What can I do for you, Monique?" I asked.

"It is not what you can do for me, ma petite. It is what I have done for you."

My forehead crinkled as I tried to think. In my defense it was late and I think I'd swallowed that last spoonful of ice cream too fast, because I had given myself an ice cream headache.

"The information about your man's mother," Monique said patiently.

Oh right, that information.

"What did you find out?" I asked curiously.

"Only what I am sure you have already surmised," said Monique.

"Spoiled brat, trust fund baby. Never held a job in her life and has spent all her adult years partying," I said. "Of course I'm just guessing."

"You would be exactly right," said Monique and I could hear the disdain in her voice. Monique had worked long and hard for years to build herself up to where she was now. She was a strong, intelligent woman who had always had a goal and she had been relentless in her ambition. A woman like Angela Copeland was anathema to everything that Monique believed in.

"Could she possibly want to get in touch with Griffin as part of some mid-life crisis?" I asked. "Maybe she has regrets about what she did and wants to make it right."

"Oh, Trudie," Monique said in that tone she uses that tells me that my simple naiveté is so appealing, yet so stupid at the same time.

"I really don't think that Angela Copeland has any regrets about the way she has lived her life. What she does have is a father who is ill."

"Griffin has a grandfather?" I said. "Neither of them have ever told me about any family other that Angela."

"I am guessing that the grandfather does not even know about Griffin. My information is that Angela has a tendency to disappear from his life on a constant basis. The people I spoke to say that chances are George Copeland does not even know that Angela was married and he definitely doesn't know about the child. My information says that if he had known there would have been a very different outcome to the situation. George Copeland is a very determined man. He would have wanted his grandson."

I understood now. It was possibly better for Lee that Angela's father had not known about the baby boy she had given birth to. At least it meant that he could raise Griffin without interference from someone with very deep pockets and the influence to go with it.

"George Copeland is currently ill. His company is looking at succession planning. A lot of the perks that Angela Copeland is so fond of come through the company," Monique said.

I understood. Angela did not want her son in her life because she regretted abandoning him. She wanted him because he had a possible economic value. I did not understand how someone could be that selfish and uncaring about her own child.

"Thank you, Monique," I said as I closed my eyes and pinched the bridge of my nose.

"If there is anything else I can do for you, Trudie, you know you only have to ask," Monique said before hanging up.

I leaned back against my couch, sighed and put the ice cream tub against my face.

Chapter Eighteen

The next morning I threw myself into my work. I was having trouble with a particular part of the recording and started downloading software to try to clean it up. I was concentrating on what I was hearing so hard that I almost missed my cell ringing from where I'd left it in my bedroom.

"Hello," I said a little breathlessly, hoping it was Griffin.

"Hello, Trudie, it's Angela."

Angela, Angela. I had to stop and think for a moment until my brain kicked in. Oh right, Angela.

"Hi, Angela, what can I do for you?" I asked, while wondering where she had found my phone number.

"I've been trying to get hold of Jake but he isn't answering the phone," she said, her voice dripping with concern.

"He's on a case at the moment," I said. "When that happens you generally don't get any contact for days." Sadly enough that was true. When there is a homicide case, minutes count. I had become used to the early morning phone calls which signaled me losing all contact with Griffin for up to a week at a time.

"Oh," said Angela regretfully. "We had so much fun yesterday, I was hoping to catch up with him again today."

Obviously Angela remembered our lunch completely differently to the way I remembered it.

"Why don't you come and meet me for a coffee?" she said cheerfully.

I really didn't want to, but I had a feeling that Griffin's mother was determined to insinuate herself into his life, however she could. With Griffin unable to be contacted, it looked like buttering up the girlfriend was the next order of business.

Sitting in the cafe that Angela had suggested, I knew this meeting had all the hallmarks of a very bad idea. Unfortunately, by the time I started to think that a phone call saying my car had broken down and I couldn't make it was in order, Angela was standing at the door, her eyes sweeping the area. When she saw me she couldn't hide the slight look of distaste. Admittedly, I hadn't exactly dressed up for her and, despite the fact I had once again tried to hide the bruising with makeup, I still looked quite the sight. Angela sat down opposite me.

"Are you sure you should be out, Trudie?" she asked, her eyes glued to the makeup that was caked onto my face.

"I got hurt during a robbery yesterday after lunch," I said. "One of those things unfortunately".

"Where do you work?"

"I'm a personal assistant. I have various clients in differing locations," I said airily, hoping that I was being appropriately vague. Despite the fact she had only just started showing an interest in her son, there was no way that I was telling the mother of my boyfriend that I was currently working at a strip club. Some things are just not meant to be shared. Lucky for me, the woman only had the ability to pretend interest in me for a very short period of time.

"I'm so glad we have this opportunity to get to know each other," Angela said as she grasped my hand on the table. "It's so important to me that I have a chance to get to know my son."

I cocked my head to one side. "Why?"

"What do you mean, why?" she said coldly, pulling her hand back. She still kept the smile going though.

"Why is it so important for you to get to know Griffin now? He's thirty years old. Surely the time to get to know your son was when he was a child and needed your hugs. Maybe when he was a teenager and needed some guidance. Those were the times when he would have welcomed his mother wanting to be a part of his life."

I knew I was probably overstepping my bounds, but I was very much afraid that this woman was going to hurt Griffin badly. If there was anyone who could hurt him, it would be his mother.

"You are being very impertinent," Angela said frostily.

Yes I was, and frankly, my mother would be appalled.

"Let me make a suggestion as to why I think you are so interested in having Jake back in your life. Your father is not well. All of a sudden he is looking at the legacy he is leaving behind and all he has is you. Considering what I've found out about your father, I am guessing there have been a few discussions between the two of you about the way you have led your life. A man that ambitious and driven would have hoped for a child with the same qualities.

Regrettably, you seem to be the complete opposite to your father, don't you? I'm guessing that inheritance issues have been coming up, so you've decided to hang in front of your father the only carrot you have. A grandson. A strong, honorable grandson, with his work ethic and determination." I shook my head. Not for the first time I wondered how this woman could possibly be Griffin's mother. "Using your son for your own economic gain is reprehensible and in this case it won't work. Griffin isn't going to be as easily manipulated as you obviously think he is."

"What would you know?" Angela hissed and I was relieved. Now I could see the real woman, not the fake one she had been presenting to us. At least now I could see who I was going to be protecting Griffin from.

"I know that Griffin doesn't need a mother who is only using him. I would suggest you find another way to get your inheritance," I said as I rose from the table.

I could feel the wave of anger aimed at my back as I walked out. I felt sick. I had just made an enemy of Griffin's mother. It may not have been the wisest decision

I made.

I was going to need some time to work out how I was going to explain to Griffin that I had completely alienated his mother. Of course, because that is the way the universe worked for me, Griffin was waiting in my apartment when I got home.

"I was just about to call you," he said waving his phone around.

"No need now," I said tightly.

"Where have you been?" Griffin asked slowly.

"Out," I said.

Griffin waited for a couple of seconds. "What's going on here, Trudie?"

"Nothing," I said brightly, wondering how long I was going to have to keep this up before he gave up and left. I should have remembered that Griffin was made of sterner stuff than that.

He sighed. "Trudie, I need you to be honest with me. Something is going on and you need to tell me what that something is, because I can't read your mind. Lord knows I wish I could because it would make my life so much easier."

It was the exasperation in his voice that got me. "I just met with your mother and now she hates me," I said.

Griffin stopped. "Why does my mother hate you? Actually no, let's start at the beginning. Why did you meet my mother? Wasn't yesterday's lunch enough of a torture for you?"

"She called me today looking for you. I told her you were working a case and she said she wanted to meet me, so I went to meet her."

"Why does she hate you?" Griffin asked.

This was the part I was not looking forward to. I sat down on the couch and waited for him to sit next to me.

"Before I start telling you this, I just want you to know that I did it with the best of intentions."

Griffin's eyes closed briefly. "What did you do?"

"After the lunch yesterday I was worried about the reason why she wanted to come back into your life all of a sudden. I asked Monique to get some information because she knows everything."

Griffin rolled his eyes at my blatant hero worship of all things Monique.

"Last night Monique called me to tell me that your grandfather is sick. Seems there may be some inheritance issues for your mother, so today I accused her of using you to get back into her father's good graces. She didn't take it too well. She didn't deny it but she wasn't too happy with me. I'm so sorry if you wanted a relationship with her and I did something that may harm that. I just hated the thought of her hurting you." I looked down at my hands twisting in my lap.

Griffin put a finger under my chin and tilted my head up until I was looking him in the eyes.

"Which part of that did you think I didn't know?" he asked gently.

I shrugged.

"As soon as Angela Copeland said she wanted to see me, I knew there had to be another angle. The woman has shown zero interest in me my entire life and all of a sudden she wants me. I found out all about her father and her life. I knew what she wanted from me before I even saw her face the first time."

I should have known. In my heedless attempt to protect him, I should have remembered that Griffin was a damn fine cop. There was no way he would go into that situation without having all the facts.

"I'm sorry," I said. "You just seem to have this problem with mothers. I thought it was because of your mom and what she did."

"What are you talking about?" Griffin asked, a little defensively.

"Your problem with moms," I said. "You don't seem to be able to cope with my mom at all. She scared you off for that couple of months when I got shot on the Eleanor Channing job." We had never discussed it but it still bothered me. It had been swept under the carpet in the midst of all our other dramas.

"I don't have problems with mothers in general," Griffin said patiently.

Really, he could have fooled me.

"I have a problem with your mother."

That wasn't good. Strangely enough I had never considered that possibility. I thought everybody adored my mother.

"Why would you have problems with my mother? She's delightful, everyone knows that," I said.

"She doesn't like me," said Griffin

That was true. She wasn't overly fond of Griffin. Unfortunately her first meeting with him had come after finding out he had blackmailed me into helping him with a murder investigation by threatening to deport me home to Australia. There was a possibility those actions may have led to me being shot. All of those facts contributed to the less than warm feelings my mother had for Griffin.

"So you don't have a problem with mothers," I said slowly.

Griffin shrugged. "No, I just don't feel particularly comfortable around your mom. After you got shot I did try to contact you, but your mom blocked me every time. I knew she blamed me for your being shot and I could tell how close the two of you are. I wanted to see you and I figured if I kept away until she left then I would have a better chance with you." He grimaced tightly. "I didn't expect the woman to stay for two months."

"Is that why you won't speak to Mom now?" I asked curiously.

Griffin looked a bit sheepish. "Your mom is scary, and there's that whole not liking me thing."

"I wouldn't say she doesn't like you," I protested.

Griffin raised an eyebrow. Okay, maybe she wasn't his

biggest fan. But I'm sure, given time, a lot of time, she would warm to him. Or at least stop glaring at him when he accidentally walked behind me during one of our Skype sessions as if she wished she had a voodoo doll and a very big pin.

"So you're telling me you feel absolutely nothing about your mother, or the fact that she left you when you were a baby, or that she is only back in your life because she wants to use you to cement her economic future."

Griffin shook his head but I'd seen the small flash of pain in his eyes. He may have been saying the words but there was still a little boy inside him who resented the fact that his mother left him. Much as Griffin maintained that his wariness around my mother was based solely on her personality, I could see there was a bit more to it. Unless he was willing to face that fact though, I wasn't going to push him. Instead I wrapped my arms around his waist and gave him a hug.

"I'm sorry I made your mother mad," I said.

He wrapped his arms around my shoulders and kissed me on the head. "I'm sorry your mother doesn't like me."

This was nice. Not the problems we both seemed to have with each other's mothers, but the fact we seemed to be getting past our issues of the last few days.

"I need you to come down to the station," Griffin said.

Moment over. Looked like we were back to work.

I tilted my head back to look up at him. "Why?"

"Ramos picked up Jayden Johnson. We need you to have a look at him."

"I didn't see anything," I protested. "My contribution to the day's events was basically opening a door, seeing Denise, seeing the gunman and then lights out."

Griffin grimaced and his eyes flew back to the bruising on my cheek.

"Still, you were the one that was assaulted."

I could tell from the way his jaw tightened as he said those words that he was really not happy with that part of the situation.

"I'll follow you in my car." I resigned myself to another day at the police station.

Chapter Nineteen

Standing in the police station, the guy who hit me looked a lot less threatening without the gun and the balaclava.

"Is there anything about him that you find familiar?" asked Ramos.

I shrugged. "I didn't see any part of him except the gun and his eyes and even then it was only for a split second. The guy reacted fast when I opened the door and I didn't react at all."

"Happens," said Ramos.

I was pretty sure it didn't happen to her. To hear Griffin tell it, Ramos was a one woman demolition team. On the plus side, it made me feel more comfortable about his job knowing he had Ramos watching his back. On the other hand, it brought home all my inadequacies whenever I spoke to her.

"I only saw his eyes for a split second. He looked shocked."

"That's okay," Ramos said, sounding disinterested.

"Why am I actually here?" I asked. "I'm no good as a witness."

"You're right there," said Ramos. "Anyway we've got some of your DNA on the gun from where it hit you."

Lovely. That still didn't answer my question. Then I saw Brandi and Susan being brought in. I smiled at them as they walked past.

"I don't believe you did that," I hissed at Ramos.

"What?" she said.

"The only reason I'm standing here is so that Brandi would see me before making a statement and her sense of guilt over my injury might encourage her to give you all the information."

Ramos looked at me speculatively. "You know, you really are smarter than you look."

"I'm leaving," I said.

"I'll let Griffin know," said Ramos.

"Don't bother. Next time you people want to play your cop mind games, at least do me the courtesy of letting me know what is going on."

As I got in my car Griffin came jogging up. "Heard you were mad," he said.

I sighed. "I'm not mad, it just would have been good if you'd told me the real reason you wanted me here."

"I was really hoping you might be able to identify the guy, but Brandi was kind of on the fence about what he'd done, especially when we started to question her about the possibility that her boyfriend may have killed Hammy Pollard. We figured seeing you and the damage he'd done to you might encourage her not to back down."

"Okay," I said.

Griffin looked perplexed. "What does that mean? Does it mean okay you understand what we did, or does it mean okay I never want to see you again?"

I shrugged. "It means okay. I understand you have a job to do and it isn't like it's the first time I've got caught in the middle of one of your cases.

Griffin cupped the side of my face. "I'm not using you. He hurt you and I just want to make sure he never gets a chance to do that again. I need to be able to put him away for as long a time as possible. Can you understand that?"

A part of me melted. At his soul, Griffin was a protector. The ugly bruise on my cheek was probably hurting him as much as it did me. "I really am okay," I said. "I think I'll just go home, do some work and rest for a bit."

Griffin lightly brushed his lips against mine. "I think that would be a good idea."

When I got home, I set up the laptop and started going through the audio files that I had downloaded from

Alistair's recorder the night before. I turned up the volume on my laptop. It sounded like Alistair had left the recorder sitting somewhere, or he was somewhere quiet and not talking to anyone. That had happened before, many times, and since it was sound activated it had at times recorded other people talking. Being uncomfortable with the situation, I had learned very quickly to only transcribe that information that I could definitely attribute to Alistair and his interviews, or the rambling monologues that doubled as his notes. I could hear muffled voices as if a discussion was happening further away, but then Hammy's voice came through the recorder quite clearly. He was angry with someone and it didn't sound like the normal Hammy annoyed with one of the girls. This argument sounded different.

"She is not going to get a cent out of this place. I worked for everything and she doesn't deserve a bit of it."

My forehead furrowed as I concentrated, trying to pick up the voice of the person he was talking to, but the voice was muffled as if whoever it was stood further away from the recorder than Hammy.

Hammy laughed. "Go back to wherever you crawled out of. You have no place here," he sneered.

I jumped when I heard a bang like someone dropping heavily to the floor and then all I could hear was a wheezing noise and scrabbling against a hard surface. I checked the time stamp on the recording. It had been recorded at the moment that Hammy had died. I blindly grabbed my cell and punched in Griffin's number.

"Trudie," he said and instantly I felt calmer.

"I need you to come to my place now," I said.

Griffin obviously heard the distress in my voice. "I'll be right there."

I sat quietly waiting for Griffin to arrive. It was one thing to know that Hammy was dead. It was another to actually hear the death throes as the man died. From what I'd heard, it hadn't been an easy death and he had fought for his life. Griffin let himself into the apartment and as he walked into my living room I could see all his senses were alert.

"What's going on, Trudie?" he said quietly as he sat down next to me.

I swallowed. "Alistair carries this small digital voice recorder everywhere he goes. He talks into the thing constantly and he uses it for interviews. It's shaped like a USB flash drive so nobody really pays any attention to it. It's sound activated so it starts recording anytime somebody talks around it. Every few days he'll give it to me to transcribe everything on it. I download the audio files to my laptop and then go through them, typing out the part of them that are relevant and not just background noise. Sometimes I use some software to clean up the noise on it."

Griffin nodded but he still looked confused.

"This is an audio file that I just started working on. It was taped on the night Hammy died."

I started playing the file.

Griffin's eyes widened. "Is that what I think it is?"

I nodded.

Griffin leaned closer. "I can't make out who the other person is. Maybe Brandi's boyfriend tried a more direct route the other night."

"I don't know," I said. "Whoever it is, they're too far away from the recorder to register their voice properly. I thought maybe you'd be able to get someone from the department to work on the file. They might be able to get something."

Griffin nodded as I downloaded a copy to a flash drive and passed it to him.

"Thanks for this, I'll let you know if it gets us anywhere," he said as he gave me a quick kiss and left, his mind already on the possibilities the file gave him.

Chapter Twenty

Trying to tackle the rest of the audio files, I kept getting distracted by the thoughts of Hammy's last moments. I wondered where Alistair had been while his recorder had been close enough to Hammy to provide a permanent account of his death. Finally, I slammed shut my laptop and headed to the office. I had a feeling Alistair knew more than he was saying. Despite his faults, of which there were many, Alistair was a formidable investigator. Before this debacle of a filmmaking exercise that I was involved in, he had made his reputation with hard hitting documentaries that had brought down corrupt government officials and greedy companies who had skirted and then dumped all over the law. Maybe he had seen something and was following it up.

When I arrived, the office was quiet. I was surprised to find that Alistair wasn't there. When he wasn't on site at the club or in meetings with lawyers, he was generally to be found in the warehouse. I think he even had a bed in a small room attached to his office. Today though, the whole place was quiet. I was starting to have a very uneasy feeling.

Sitting down at my desk I logged on my computer. When I first started working with Alistair he had given me network access to all his research notes. I went in to the research notes on the club and found a folder titled Hammy. Opening it up, I found the photo of Denise and Hammy on their wedding day. Now that I looked at it closely I could see the slight baby bump under the wedding dress. I wondered if she had given up the baby for Hammy. I couldn't even begin to imagine how that would feel.

Looking out the window, I noticed something small sitting on the ledge. As I went over to the window I could see that it was Alistair's recorder.

Looking down at it in my hand, I made a decision and downloaded it onto my computer. I could see that Alistair had created a few new files since I gave the recorder back to him the previous night. Throwing on my headphones, I listened to Alistair's voice. He had been putting something together. It seemed that he had become aware of the change that Hammy had been planning to make with his will. He had plenty of theories as to why Hammy might have been killed. Unfortunately he didn't have much in the way of evidence. The folder did show that he was investigating and Alistair did have a reputation for being relentless.

When I opened the last file I was surprised to hear Amber's voice in the background.

"What are you doing here, Amber?" Alistair growled. I could hear the sound of the recorder being placed on a hard surface.

"I just wanted to see you," purred Amber.

Hearing the seductive tone in her voice, I suddenly felt uncomfortable. I had believed that Amber was no longer interested in Alistair and his lies. Obviously I'd been wrong.

"I'm busy, Amber, I've got something I'm looking into." Alistair sounded distracted.

Amber sighed. "I was afraid you would say that." Her voice had suddenly become hard. "Alistair, Alistair, you really shouldn't have started sticking your nose in where it wasn't wanted. That kind of thing can get you into a lot of trouble. You do know that, don't you?"

"Amber, just leave. I'll see you later when I've got time."

Alistair sounded dismissive to the woman he had been sleeping with. That was Alistair, sensitive to the end.

"You really shouldn't turn your back on me," hissed

Amber.

The next thing I heard was a thud. "And you really need to reevaluate the way you treat women," said Amber with a cheery note in her voice. There was silence and then I heard Amber's voice again. "We've got a problem, Mom. I'll be there in a little while but I'm going to need some help."

Hearing the dragging noise, I ripped off the headphones and grabbed the recorder. Heading for the door, I pulled up short when Amber stepped through it.

"Hi, Trudie," she said, smiling brightly.

"Hi, Amber," I replied, trying to smile just as brightly. Proving once again why my childhood dreams of becoming an actress never had any chance of coming to fruition, Amber's eyes darkened.

"You look nervous," she said suspiciously. "Has something happened?"

"No, no. I've just been doing some work and Alistair left me a list of errands that he wants me to run."

Amber's eyes narrowed in on the hand holding the recorder and realization crossed her face.

"Oh, Trudie, this is unfortunate," she said.

I stepped back. "What do you mean?" I knew my voice was a little high pitched but there was really nothing that I could do about it.

"You know, don't you?" she said. She didn't come towards me but she was blocking off the doorway.

It's amazing how sometimes, moments of pure terror can clear your mind and you can see things that haven't been obvious before. I usually saw Amber at the club with her makeup and costume on. Today though, she was completely natural and I saw something different.

"You're Denise's daughter aren't you?"

I should have seen it earlier. Now that the pieces were falling into place, I could see the similarities. Amber had the same chin and nose as her mother. If the situation hadn't been so unexpected, I might have spotted it earlier.

Amber looked at me sadly. "You really should have kept out of this, Trudie," she said. Her eyes flicked behind me and pain exploded in the back of my head.

Chapter Twenty-One

For the first time in a while I made my way out of unconsciousness without Dominic Caldwell looking down on me. For a brief and admittedly insane moment I missed him. My only excuse was that while I had been realizing that Amber was not quite the innocent stripper dominatrix that she appeared, somebody had sneaked up behind me and cracked me in the back of the head with something hard. That may have messed with my thinking processes somewhat. I would also like to point out that hitting me in the back of the head while there was a slight possibility that I was already suffering from concussion was a really lousy way to do things.

"Trudie, is that you?"

Now that was not fair. It wasn't enough that I had been kidnapped. It looked like I'd been kidnapped to keep Alistair company.

I groaned as I turned my head. Sure enough, there was Alistair sitting with his back against the wall.

"What happened?" I croaked as I struggled to sit up.

"We've been kidnapped," muttered Alistair.

Well, thank you Captain Obvious. I would have thought, being a hard hitting seeker of the truth, as I had actually heard him describe himself once, that I would have got a bit more detail regarding our predicament.

"This is all your fault," he accused.

I was used to the many ways perspective could be shifted in Hollywood. A drug overdose could actually be exhaustion and picking up a prostitute was the act of a good samaritan. Even knowing that, I failed to see how this was in any way, shape or form, my fault. I was not the one who had the bright idea of filming a documentary in a strip club. I was not the one who decided that a skeleton crew of three was the best way to film the documentary. I was not the one sleeping with the person who had kidnapped us. If anything, the only mistake that I had made was answering the phone the day Monique called and offered me a job working for a man who had managed to alienate every single person who had ever been in his employ.

I'd been kidnapped before, on my own, by a dangerous man and then passed along to another very dangerous man. At the time I thought that, although I wouldn't wish for anyone else to be kidnapped with me, it would have been good not to go through it alone. Logically you would assume having someone with you when you've been kidnapped, who wasn't one of the kidnappers, would be a good thing. I was quickly finding out that that was not true. If I had been given a choice of being kidnapped on my own or being kidnapped with Alistair, I would have definitely chosen on my own.

"Where are we?" I asked, choosing to ignore Alistair's accusation.

"I don't know," he said. "She hit me on the head, how could she do that?"

He was honestly perplexed. How wonderful must it be to live in your own world where there are no consequences to your actions.

I slowly rose to my feet and looked around. Wherever we were, it was dark. There was some light coming from underneath a doorway. I tried the handle but the door didn't give.

"Because that wouldn't be the first thing I'd try," said Alistair sarcastically.

Definitely having fond memories of the times I'd been kidnapped on my own. I banged on the door and yelled. "Is anyone out there?"

As the door came open I took a step back, only to be confronted by a smiling Amber. Following her were Denise and to my surprise, Hugh. I stepped towards

Alistair as they came into the room.

"Oh good, you're awake" she said, smiling.

I would have taken some comfort in that statement, believing if she was going to kill me she would have done it already. Unfortunately I could see the distressed looks on Denise and Hugh's faces. I had a very bad feeling that they didn't have a vote in this decision.

"Why are you doing this, Amber?" I asked, watching her walk around Alistair and me as if we were art pieces in a gallery.

"I'm taking back control," said Amber. "Did you know he forced our mother to give my brother and me away?"

I slid my eyes over to Hugh. Twins. "You were the one who hit me." It was more of a statement than a question. I should have known. With his ability to sneak up on someone, I hadn't stood a chance.

Hugh nodded. "Sorry I had to do that."

"Could have been worse," giggled Amber. "You should see his skills with a whip."

I was surprised but I shouldn't have been. Amber had been on stage when Hammy died, Denise had been at a church meeting. The owner of the murder weapon and the one who had the most to gain had great alibis. Who would have suspected the man who had no investment in Hammy's life whatsoever? It was brilliant, in a completely crazy kind of way.

"You killed your father to get hold of the club," I said.

"He owed it to us," said Amber. "We were tossed aside as if we were nothing because he liked this life so much. Hugh and I grew up never knowing our family, all because of him. We had a plan in place to make it look like an accident. It was brilliant, but then he changed his will to give this place to the crying girl. We couldn't let that happen so we had to improvise."

And improvising meant strangling a man with a whip. I had to stop myself from shuddering. This was a serious conspiracy happening here. It was interesting to see that

Denise and Hugh did not seem to have the same enthusiasm for this situation that Amber did. Amber was acting like she was in Disneyland. It concerned me that I had not seen this level of crazy in her before. I shook my head.

"It isn't like Hammy was living the high life here. The man was in debt up to his eyeballs."

"That's where Alistair came in with his big plans and all that money," said Amber and she brushed her lips across Alistair's cheek as she walked past him.

I had to give Alistair credit. He was standing straight and tall. He wasn't even flinching at the realization that he had been involved with a woman, not only capable of planning the death of her father, but seemingly eager to do it.

"If you had this master plan," sneered Alistair, finally finding his voice. "Why did you get involved with me?"

I couldn't believe it. I actually heard a little bit of hurt in his voice as if he was affronted that she may have used him.

"Would you believe Hammy wanted me to keep you happy? He saw that you were interested and he so wanted you to keep paying him. It worked in well with our plans. Bring the money in and then get the club. And you were so easy. As long as you thought you had all the power. That's the aim of the best seductions," Amber said, as she stroked the side of Alistair's face and looked over at me as if imparting the wisdom of the ages. "If they believe that they always have the upper hand, they will never know that you are using them."

Despite the fact that everything in me said that Amber was a few sandwiches short of a picnic, you had to admire her ability to stay on task.

"You have no problem with this, Denise?" I asked, hoping to find an ally.

"I'm sorry, Trudie. You seem like a nice girl but this reckoning was a long time coming. I lost my babies because of him. I've only just found them. I can't risk losing them again."

Hugh nodded in agreement.

Amber came up beside me. "They're not going to help you, Trudie. You got in the way. That was a very bad idea. You really need to learn to mind your own business. Everything would have worked out perfectly if you and Alistair had simply stuck to your roles."

"What are you going to do with us?" And by us I meant me because at that point I found it really difficult to care one bit regarding her plans for Alistair.

"Well," said Amber brightly. "Unfortunately we can't do anything right now, the club is about to open and things could get a bit messy. I just need you to settle in and be patient. Once the club closes we'll take care of everything."

Alistair's jaw dropped and he looked completely horrified. I had to admit that I was feeling slightly sick myself. I don't think there was any doubt as to how Amber was planning to take care of everything. As the three of them left and the door closed I heard a bolt sliding into place.

"We're in the club somewhere," I said to Alistair without looking around.

I heard a thump behind me. I spun around to find Alistair had slumped to the floor and was holding his head in his hands.

"Did you hear her?" he moaned. "She's going to kill me."

I liked that he didn't really seem to care that I was also going to be included in that equation. I squatted down next to him.

"Alistair, you were the one who researched this place. Do you know where we are?"

"She's going to kill me," he repeated. Obviously Alistair was unable to multitask at this point in time. It seemed the news of his impending death had taken over his entire brain, leaving no room for the possibility of escape.

"Alistair, I need you to focus. Do you know where in the club we are?" I said it as clearly and slowly as I could and was rewarded when he looked up at me.

"We're in the basement. We are going to die in the basement of a strip club."

Well that was clear enough for me. I looked around. The basement was small and as far as I could see, there didn't seem to be any way of getting out of it without first going through that door.

"Maybe there's a weapon we could use, you know, to take her out when she comes back for us." Alistair raised his head and smiled. Of course it wasn't a nice smile. In point of fact it pretty much matched Amber's smile, but seeing as how it was on my side now, I was a lot less bothered by it.

I clapped him on the back. "Brilliant plan, now we just need to find something."

Strangely enough, the basement of a strip club did not exactly lend itself to finding weapons. We found a lot of old costumes that looked like they had seen better days and bottles of caked makeup. Looking in a closet I found a large tin.

"Maybe we could use this?" I said, showing Alistair.

The look he gave me spoke volumes. He was right, as far as weapons went, it didn't really have the impact we were hoping for. Unfortunately this basement looked like it wasn't used for much in the way of storage at all. I shook the tin. Hearing something inside, I opened it up and found a sheaf of papers.

"Alistair," I said.

"You're wasting my time," said Alistair. "Unless you've found something useful, don't bother me."

At that moment if I'd found something useful I would have used it on him.

"I've found the will," I said.

"What?" said Alistair, coming up beside me.

"I've found the will leaving the club to Brandi and it's been signed."

"Fascinating as that is, I don't see how it could possibly help us out of this mess," Alistair said, resuming his hunt for a weapon.

We both froze as we heard the bolt slide back. Alistair grabbed the tin out of my hand and strode towards the door. I followed him to back him up. As a figure came through the door Alistair held the tin high in the air and brought it down hard. I grabbed his arm just before it connected when I realized that the person opening the door was not one of Hammy's demented family, but was Brandi.

"What are you doing here?" I hissed.

"Who cares," said Alistair. "The door is open, I'm leaving now."

"I heard Amber talking," said Brandi, swallowing nervously. "I called Susan and she said she'd get help."

"We need to get out of here now," I said to Brandi. "Is there anyone backstage?"

Brandi shook her head. "Denise is having a meeting. Amber and Hugh are out the front."

"Let's go," I said. "We'll go out the back."

"Finally," growled Alistair.

Chapter Twenty-Two

As we made our way through the back hallway, we were surprised when Denise and Dominic walked out of Hammy's office. I pushed Brandi and Alistair forward. Denise hadn't seen us yet and with any luck we could hide in the alcove until they went past.

"Trudie, such a pleasure to see you here," boomed Dominic.

I closed my eyes. Once again I had that horrible feeling in the pit of my stomach that Dominic Caldwell was going to get me killed.

Denise's eyes widened.

"Go," I whispered to Brandi and Alistair.

Brandi scampered away and I hoped that she would get help. Alistair, proving that sometimes people surprise you, stayed with me and we both turned around.

"Hi, Dominic, it is so good to see you. I really would love to stay and chat with you but I've just got to pop out for a bit. Can we please catch up later today?"

I could see the confusion on Dominic's face. Our interactions previously had consisted of me being quite brutally honest with my desire to stay as far away from him as possible. Actually suggesting that I wanted his company was as far from my normal behavior as we could possibly get. I hoped he got the message.

I heard a swift intake of breath from Alistair and looked over. There, standing next to him, was Amber and I could see that she was carrying a large knife which now pressed very firmly into Alistair's side.

"Now," she said with that smile that I knew, if I survived this, was going to give me nightmares for weeks. "I think we all need to calm down and think things through for the next few moments."

I was thinking. At this moment my mind was racing. Despite the fact I was still relatively free, I couldn't leave Alistair, because I could see from the look in Amber's eyes that she was quite capable of killing him where he stood. Despite my questionable past, I had not yet lost a client and I wasn't going to start with Alistair, tempting though the thought may have been at times.

"What are you doing, sweetheart?" asked Denise.

She looked nervous and kept glancing at Dominic. I didn't blame her. Dominic was the unknown quantity here. My personal hope was that we had enough of a relationship that he might have a vested interest in my continued survival.

At that point Hugh walked into the hallway.

"What's happening here?" he asked slowly.

"It seems Alistair and Trudie didn't have the patience to wait like I asked them to," said Amber, twisting the knife in Alistair's side with every word.

"I feel I've missed something," mused Dominic.

I doubted it, but I was so completely out of options that I was willing to follow wherever he was going.

"Amber and Hugh here are Denise's children who Hammy made her give up when she got pregnant. They are the ones who killed Hammy."

There, everyone was up to date. Now I just needed Dominic to do whatever he planned to do to get us out of this.

"That was messy," remarked Dominic. "If you're going to kill somebody there really shouldn't be a body left behind. It does make things inconvenient."

Of course. I expected a brilliant rescue plan, what I get is Murder 101 for psychopaths. If it was possible, Alistair looked even more horrified than I did.

"You've really made quite the mess of things haven't you?" said Dominic as he casually strolled over to my side. "I wish I could help you, but unfortunately for you, I am quite fond of Trudie."

I was never going to admit how happy that sentiment made me feel right at this point in time.

Dominic placed his hand under my elbow. "Now if you will excuse me, I will be taking Trudie and we will be walking out of here."

Amber looked at him as if he was crazy.

"What about Alistair?" I hissed. Alistair looked at us as if to agree.

"I don't care about Alistair," Dominic said, totally unconcerned with Alistair's plight.

"I'm going to kill him," Amber threatened.

Alistair whimpered and Dominic rolled his eyes.

"How do you get yourself into these situations?" he asked me.

"Police," yelled out Griffin from the doorway, where he and Ramos were standing with guns raised.

"Finally," said Dominic.

"No," said Amber, pushing the knife into Alistair a little bit harder. "It wasn't supposed to be like this. The club belongs to us. We earned it."

"No it doesn't," I said. "We found the will leaving the place to Brandi."

Amber faltered. "No, that isn't possible. We can't have gone through all this just for him to leave it to her."

"Miss," said Griffin. "Put the knife down now or we will shoot you."

Amber looked down at the knife that she had digging into Alistair's side, indecision in her eyes. I could see she was tempted to push the blade in and I held my breath. I let the breath out when I heard the clatter of the knife as it hit the floor.

"Everyone on your knees," yelled Ramos.

Dominic pulled me aside as the area filled with police. Amber, Hugh and Denise ended up in handcuffs, glaring resentfully at me. Not unexpectedly, Alistair had the same look.

"I don't think I'll be requiring your services anymore,"

he said to me stiffly before being ushered away by paramedics wanting to look at his side.

Once again I was tempted to remind him that he wasn't technically my employer, his manager was. That being said, I had a feeling that my time with Alistair had reached its natural conclusion.

"So you're unemployed?" said Dominic.

"No," I sighed. "I do not want to work for you and I fail to see why you would possibly want me in your employ. This is the second time you and I have been in a hostage situation and we don't even live in the same city. Could you imagine what would happen if I worked for you?"

Dominic gave an unabashed grin and for a moment I could see why so many women were willing to ignore his reputation. "I think it would be fun."

Some people had the weirdest definition of fun.

Griffin walked over to us and glared at Dominic.

"I'll wait over there," Dominic said.

Griffin waited until we were alone.

"Are you hurt?" he asked.

"I got hit on the head again," I said. "And I got kidnapped, again."

Griffin stroked my hair back and tucked it behind my ear.

"I want you to get checked by the paramedics and we need a statement," he said.

"Okay," I replied.

Griffin smiled. "No argument, it must be my lucky day."

"I'm too tired to argue," I said.

Brandi came up to me and I smiled. "You did great Brandi. Thank you so much, you saved our lives."

Brandi beamed.

"This is yours," I said as I passed the paper I had hidden in the waistband of my pants.

"What is it?" asked Brandi, looking confused.

"It's the will Hammy showed you. It looks like he did sign it before he died," I said.

"You mean I own this place," Brandi gasped.

I nodded and pointed over to Dominic. "You see that man over there. The estate owes him some money but I really think he might buy this place from you, just make sure you have a lawyer look through the deal before signing anything. You can leave and make a new start, somewhere far away from here."

Brandi's eyes filled with tears. "Thank you," she gasped, before making her way over to Dominic.

"You ready?" said Griffin.

I nodded and leaned into him as he put his arm around me.

Chapter Twenty-Three

L ying in my bed later that night, I had trouble getting to sleep. As expected, that smile of Amber's that was filled with hatred for her father, was dancing in front of my eyes every time I closed them. After giving my statement to Ramos and being given the all clear by the paramedics, I had been shipped home in the care of one of the obliging uniformed officers.

I heard Griffin come into my apartment and he stopped at my bedroom door.

"Am I still welcome to come in?" he asked.

I sighed and sat up, clicking on the lamp sitting on my bedside table. "Of course you are."

"Can't sleep?" asked Griffin as he sat down on the bed beside me.

I shook my head. "How did it go?"

"The three of them are turning on each other like sharks in a feeding frenzy. According to each of them it was the other's idea. The kids are mostly blaming Denise. From the sounds of it there seems to be a lot of resentment that has built up over the fact that she chose to give them away so that she wouldn't lose Hammy. It seems Amber's real name is Janine Eaton." He looked at me expectantly as if thinking I'd be shocked that I didn't even know her real name, because I obviously truly believed that these girls were all born with names like Amber and Brandi. I had become very comfortable early on with the fact I would never know the real names of these girls. "Seems Amber is really a paralegal from Wisconsin. She tracked down her mother and then the two of them managed to track down her brother. Seems this family had skills in strategy. Amber went and got a job at the club. Hugh was already working for Alistair and managed to talk him into doing the documentary there."

So Alistair wasn't the narcissistic jerk who thought making an exploitative feature on the lives of strippers was a way to win his next award. He was a gullible idiot who was obviously easily led.

"They had everything in place. The idea was to get as much of the club paid off as quickly as they could and then kill him. Very clinical plan. Hugh saw Hammy tell Brandi about the will on some of the camera footage and plans had to be moved up a bit. The whole thing hinged on Denise still inheriting the club. Brandi threw a major complication into the works. Hugh was the one who actually killed Hammy. We managed to clean up the audio file enough to get that information. Seems he tried to talk Hammy out of changing the will first. Looks like Hugh was a bit reluctant to actually kill his father, but he had his orders. If I had to put money on it I would think that Amber was the mastermind behind it. Denise seems to still be carrying a lot of guilt about giving her kids up. Hugh has some resentment but he doesn't have the true anger required. He might have been the one who actually killed Hammy, but Amber was the one who pushed the whole plan forward. That woman is a seething mass of hate for her father."

I was no longer surprised.

Griffin cleared his throat. "I owe you an apology."

I stayed silent, waiting for him to continue.

Griffin shook his head. "The things I said to you about Travis were unfair and I should never have said them."

"I don't understand why you would have said those things. I would never do anything like that to you," I said. "I need to understand where that came from."

I could see Griffin swallow nervously. "I screwed up because I was scared. When Travis and I were partners there was an incident. We were chasing some kid who was hyped up on drugs. We got separated. When I found Travis again the kid was dead. Coroner said that he died from a blow to the head, consistent with hitting his head on the ground after being struck. I was the one who had to notify the kid's parents. I had to look his mother in the face and tell her that her son wasn't ever coming home again. She was a wreck and I was pretty raw when Internal Affairs interviewed me. They asked me if I could have found another way to deal with the kid, in the state he was in. At the time I thought there had to be a way that Travis could have dealt with the situation, where this kid didn't end up dead. I should have told them that there wasn't. I know that Travis would have done everything to save that kid. I didn't back him up and he lost his career over it. I know they cleared him, but my not backing him one hundred percent put a cloud over him that he couldn't live with and it's why he's no longer a cop. I know he loved being a cop and I destroyed his career."

Griffin's remorse was palpable. "Maybe you need to talk to him about it," I suggested. "It would probably help him a lot to know all this."

Griffin nodded. "I will. I think it's time for this to be dealt with."

"I understand your guilt when it comes to Travis, but how does that relate to me?" I asked.

Griffin smiled gently. "Because of me, Travis lost the thing he loved the most, being a cop. I was afraid that he'd found a way to get his revenge by taking away what I love the most."

I stopped breathing for a moment and Griffin tilted my chin up so I was looking deep into those emerald green eyes.

"I love you, Trudie. You mean more to me than anything else in my life. The thought of losing you absolutely terrifies me. I am so sorry for what I said. I never, ever, for one instant really thought that you would do anything like that, but I was scared. I couldn't bear the thought of losing you. I didn't realize that I was actually pushing you away. I am so sorry. I just can't lose you."

I blinked back the tears that were welling in my eyes and he brushed his lips against mine.

"Promise me that you are going to stay safe. Promise me that you will never get into a situation like today again," Griffin pleaded.

I really and truly wished I could, but my Grandma Rita always told me to never make a promise unless you truly believe that you could keep it. I wanted to make that promise, I really did, but the way my life went, I really didn't think it was a good idea to tempt fate, so I did the next best thing.

"I love you too."

About The Author

Leonie Gant started her writing career at the age of ten when she stuffed notes in her pencil case full of ideas for mysteries that Nancy Drew and the Hardy Boys should really have been solving. After years of watching mysteries play out in her head, she decided that writing them down was the best way to deal with them.

In her life away from writing, she is a voracious reader with not nearly enough time to make her way through all the books that she wants to read. She enjoys bushwalking, sewing and chocolate, possibly not in that order. She also believes in the value of trying new things, walking in the rain and enjoying every moment.

To find out more about Leonie Gant and her books
www.leoniegant.com

Discover other titles by Leonie Gant
Not Famous in Hollywood
Not Happily Married in Hollywood
Not Talented in Hollywood
Not Suspicious in Hollywood
Not Forgotten in Hollywood